The Resolute Heart

by

Beatrice Hale,

Aberdeen Quine

Thank you to my family for all their love,

help and support.

CHAPTER ONE

May 1805. A peeping sun lit the grey streets of Sillery in Fife, on the east coast of Scotland. It sent shafts of light across the houses of the small fishing village and glinted on the sea. It danced over a small group of fishermen, their boots slipping on the cobblestones, struggling with a band of men in uniform. It shone on their assailants, some dozen determined sailors with pistols and cutlasses.

The Press Gang was at work. More men were needed to defend Britain against Napoleon's navy. And fishermen, who were also experienced sailors, were just what was wanted. So the Admiralty sent a gang of sailors to grab any seaman or any able-bodied man they could get. The fishing villages of Fife were a perfect hunting ground.

'Mary! Mary!'

The name was a scream from several people, barely heard above pounding feet, the clash of steel, yells of men, jostling and thrusting through the main street of Sillery.

Mary Watson, coming out of a neighbour's house, picked up her skirts and ran into the street. Harry, her husband, was struggling with three men. His cap had fallen off his red head, his thick woollen jersey was half off his shoulders, and his boots scrabbled for a foothold on the cobbled street. Two men held his arms and were pulling him along. The third was pushing him and trying to drag another man at the same time. She recognised Harry's friend, Jock.

'Harry!' she shouted. 'Harry! Harry! Jock!' She ran awkwardly after the group, stumbling on the cobblestones. Other men were being dragged off too, held captive by the sailors, yelling and fighting against their captors.

'Out of the way! Out of the way! Move! Go on! Move!' A man's harsh voice sounded in her ears, as did the clattering hooves of the horse he rode – too close!

Mary felt the horse's powerful shoulders pressing against her. She turned and tried to shove the animal away, pushing at his well-muscled forequarter, trying to force him back. The animal snorted and tossed his head to free himself from her obstructing hand. A slashing whip thrashed down on her arm and shoulder. She screamed as her numbed right hand dropped from the horse's neck, and she cradled it in her left hand, the pain of the wounds penetrating deep into her arm and spreading to her shoulder. Blood oozed through the cuts in her sleeve.

She glared up into the fierce grey eyes, the grim, thin-lipped mouth and jutting chin of the rider, a lieutenant, by the look of his uniform. She thought she recognised him, but she was in no state to work it out. His upper face was shadowed by his hat-brim, a sword at his side, his right hand on the reins, and the other holding the whip. He glared back at her, leaning down to grab her right shoulder with his whip hand and began to drag her along with him. Another captive? He couldn't want a woman in the navy – he was trying to frighten her. In pain, and angry as well as terrified, she struggled to pull her arm from his grasp, and pushing with her other hand at the horse. At last she managed to wrench her shoulder free, and slithered past the horse, dodging its lashing tail.

'Harry!' she shouted again, seeing his red head disappear round the corner among the struggling throng. She had to follow.

But the horseman was not minded to let her go. He nudged his horse forward with his heels, and its left forequarter caught Mary again on her right side, pushing her along, sidling close to her, so that she staggered, slipping on the cobblestones. To save herself from a fall under the horse's hooves, she flung out her hand, felt it scraping along the belly towards the stirrup. Her sleeve caught in the stirrup iron and with the horse's movement, her wrist was twisted across to the terrifying spurs on the shining leather of the rider's heel. He swung his boot back, pulling her trapped arm with him. His powerful thighs guided the horse forward, pushing her back towards its tail, her feet slipping again on the cobblestones. She clenched her fingers and tore her sleeve free. Her fist caught in the hem of the long coatee, and she grabbed it with her other hand to help her balance. Her grip slackened as the horse moved on. She clutched harder at the coatee and felt the inner material tear under her fingers. The rider pulled free and kicked her off with his spurred heel as he moved towards the pressed men. She stumbled again on the kerb and fell, gasping.

'Hey! Hoy! You great bully! Leave the women alone. Leave us be!' A yell from behind the horse and a rain of stones aimed at the horse's side came swinging past Mary. She struggled to her feet, looking round. An old woman had her arm up, hand back ready to swing into action and throw more stones. 'Grannie! Grannie Watson! Don't!' Mary grabbed the arm, forcing it down, and prising open the old hand holding the stones. 'He'll kill us, he'll kill us! Don't yell like that. Don't throw the stones. Don't.'

'What a hirdum-dirdum! Give me more! I'll

see them off.' The old woman swung her arm back again, ready to throw. Mary grabbed the thick fleshy arm and shoved it down again, squeezing the hand open to release the stones. The old woman shrieked in fury.

But the rider had lost interest in them. Attracted by noise from the crowd at the quay the rider turned his horse away. Old Grannie Watson picked up a bigger stone. It hit the horse squarely on its flanks, and the creature reared, its metal shoes clanking and sliding on the cobbles. The man swore furiously, but he could do nothing until he controlled his animal. Mary tugged urgently at Harry's grandmother's arm, pulling her back before the rider could turn on her. The horse was still pawing the air with sharp hooves. Small children were screaming and scrambling into the doorways of houses and shops, women were running after them, grabbing them and dragging them away from the danger. The narrow main street was full of tramping feet, men thrusting through, a couple of big horses now moving amongst the crowd. Above all the noise the shouts of the pressed men sounded in the air.

'We'll be back, we'll be back.'

Mary clutched Grannie Watson firmly and pushed her back through the oncoming crowd. Once clear, she was almost surprised to see that the sun still shone along the corridors of sky made by the pointed roofs of the houses thrusting upwards.

Mary helped old Grannie Watson to her house, aware her hand still held some stones. Harry's mother, Maggie, was standing at the door, face white with shock, her hands twisting her apron into a knot she'd find hard to undo later on.

'What's happening? Is that the press gang? They're no allowed! What are we going to do? Who'll help us? He's away. He's away! They've taken him.' It came out as a low, continuous moan, already full of pain.

Mary helped old Grannie Watson up the sandstone steps into the house. The door opened into a small hallway and then into the kitchen with its crackling coal fire, and the big bed behind the curtains. Mary settled Grannie, now calmer, into her seat by the fire. Maggie still stood at the door.

'They've taken my Harry. Where's he goin'? They've taken him.'

Mary pulled her gently back into the warm house. Maggie had lost her husband several years ago, a fisherman drowned in a stormy sea. Was she going to lose her son as well? Shivering, Maggie moved slowly towards the fireplace, and seized the poker. Grannie Watson leaned back in her chair as Maggie slammed the poker down on the glowing coals. Mary watched her smashing the fire, the precious coal in bits, so that it burned brightly, but too quickly. Already Mary could see the ash forming. Maggie was in a dwam, face drawn, eyes staring. She turned blindly, as Mary gently touched her arm and pulled her into a hug.

The stiff lips whispered.

'My boy, my boy. Oh, my laddie, where have they taken you to?'

And at last she started to sob. Mary stood, still hugging, while the sobbing continued. Her arm ached, her shoulder ached, and she felt a dampness on her sleeve, suggesting the blood was still oozing out of the cuts.

Gradually the sobbing ceased, and Maggie stood back, wiping her face, slowly bringing herself to life again. She pointed at some blood on Mary's wrist, oozing down from her arm.

'Let's have a wee look.'

'Aye, but I'll have to go.'

'You'll need to wash off that blood first.'

Mary raised her arm with some difficulty, and both Maggie and old Grannie could see it as Maggie pushed back her sleeve. Grannie gasped when she saw the long cut where the whip had slashed into her arm, but Maggie had returned to her practical self, though her shoulders were stiff with the effort. Seeing that Mary was in a hurry, she quickly poured water from the kettle into a basin, and Mary wiped her wounds, dabbing them dry. Maggie turned away to find some cloths for bandages.

'It's not so deep. The blood's beginning to stop.' Mary wound the rag Maggie had given her round her arm, and pulled her sleeve over it. She turned and faced Harry's mother.

'I have to go back, Ma, to see where they're going.' Maggie made a quick gesture, ready to hold her back, but Mary shook her head, and pulled away. 'I have to go, I have to go and find where they're takin' our men.' She turned from the bleak atmosphere in the kitchen and ran outside again, slamming the door as she jumped down the steps. Her arm was painful, but the blood was clotting, thanks to the rag she'd wound round the wounds.

Mary ran back through the town. She saw the horse, its tail flailing from side to side, driving the press gang and its captives onward. The crowd had held them back. Women still clutched at the sailors' backs, yelling, 'Leave him be! Leave him be!'

She saw the Provost, the town's magistrate, coming out on to the sea front with a paper in his hand.

'Stop! This is illegal. You are forbidden to

take men in the fishing industry!'

His words could barely be heard above the noise of the struggle. He tried again.

'*Stop! We will arrest you.*'

The lieutenant raised his sword, and turned his horse towards the Provost.

'NO!' The scream went all round the streets. 'NO! STOP! NO! NO!'

It was her own voice screaming. She found herself diving across the cobbles to reach the horse, flinging herself against its mighty side. The horse lunged and pivoted, and once again the rider had to pull it under control.

He spun on his horse, the sun glinting on the sword blade. His mouth was drawn back in a yell of fury.

'*Get out of my way, you jaud!*'

That face … she was sure she had seen before in Sillery. But who was he?

But before she could think, she gasped. He had turned his horse's flanks to squeeze her up against a stone wall. The hooves were brushing against her boots, the strong hind legs and heavy flank pressing her body into the stonework. Again! This fight was the same as before! Some trick he had learned, no doubt, she thought, but the smell of horse and leather was strong in her face again, almost in her mouth. And again, the metal of the stirrups dug into her body, and the spurs on the boot rowelled her clothes, piercing the skin beneath. Her hands pushed vainly against the horse's belly as the movements brought it nearer and nearer, pressing her harder against the wall so she could scarcely breathe. The grey flank moved closer, the hooves clopping on the stones, the shining spur on the boot, the muddy stirrup and the heavy heel were now within inches of her face. She looked up and saw a sword blade aimed straight at her heart.

Some instinct of fury brought her hand up and she shoved the blade aside with the back of her arm. The movement brought the booted spur further into her bodice, piercing her skin again. The fist holding the sword pommel swiped, but caught the edge of her bonnet, shoving it brutally back, the ribbons strained against her throat.

Anger pushed fear away. With the horse's smell in her nostrils, his flanks pushing the breath from her body, still she reached out to pummel the horse's belly, stretched to pull at the girths, and drove her fist into the man's leg just above the boot. He leaned over sideways to push her off and she grabbed with both hands at his coat as she was dragged off her feet. In her struggles to keep her footing, she clutched hard at the coat's tails. Inside the tails were small pockets. There was a tearing sound, and a corner of the inside pocket ripped from the lining. Something was loose inside it. She could see two papers, folded and stuck together, pushed into the pocket lining. The lining shifted and tore as she clung on to the coat. And both papers fell on to the ground. No one else noticed, not even the horseman himself.

Someone squeezed himself in front of her and shoved at the horse's flank, forcing it back. Relieved of the pressure, she slid down the wall. The cobblestones thumped into her side as she hit the ground. Blood was trickling through her bodice. She tried to staunch the blood with her tucker, and peered up and sideways. The older men of the town had their hands on the horse's bridle, pulling it forward. Another man grabbed at the horseman's legs, distracting the officer's aim. Wrenching free, the horseman lashed out with his sword and drove his spurs into the creature's sides. The man screamed as the blade caught his shoulder. The noise and the pain from the spurs made the great beast rear. The men were thrown aside.

'He got me, the great lout. He got me in the shoulder.'

The rider calmed his horse once again, and moved off. Mary stretched to pick up the thick paper from the ground. The second piece was stuck by a corner to the first. She'd keep these, she thought –

who knew what was in it? As she did so, another hand grabbed at the larger piece of paper and succeeded in tearing off a strip. Mary tried to grab the torn strip back. Now she had part of it, she wanted the whole paper, though she had no idea why. Whoever had tried to snatch it from her had given up, moved away.

As she struggled from the ground, she tried to see who it had been. She stared round the crowd. A blue-coated man was moving away from her. Tall, dark-haired, and his hand was just pushing something into the pocket of his waistcoat. She could see no more than that. She willed him to turn round and, as if he'd heard her thoughts, he swivelled his head to gaze behind him, perhaps at her, she thought. She could see a straight profile, a chin thrust forward, a look of authority. She tucked the papers quickly up her sleeve, out of sight.

Someone stooped to help her get up. Her feet scrabbled for a hold on the ground. Her arm aching and her dress torn, she struggled to her feet. Once upright, Mary turned to thank her rescuer – her neighbour Jeannie, Jock's wife.

'They've got your Harry and Jock's off as well.'

'How many?'

'Just the three or four, I'm thinking.'

So at least some of the other young men had managed to escape. That would mean a lot to the little village, who needed the strength of the younger men for the fishing, sailing the small craft on the rough seas, hauling the heavy nets, and getting the catch back to shore.

Mary and Jeannie ran over the rough ground towards the jetty as the pressed men were pushed along by the horseman and the press gang. As Mary watched the men were force-marched on board a big rowing boat. There were other men in the boat. Mary didn't know them. Most likely she thought, they're from Crail or Anstruther. So, the press was working its way up and down the coast, needing men to fill the ships. Rumour had it that the French were gathering a great fleet and Britain was to make sure that she had as many ships, if not more, to be ready to repel the French and Spanish invasion. So, men were needed!

She forced back her tears, narrowing her eyes, trying to fix every moment of the scene in her brain. Her fists were crammed into her open mouth, to stifle the shout, as Harry, hands tied, tried to raise them to signal to her. Hands tied? Harry? That meant he had been fighting hard. His red hair was scuffed over his brow, his face was white as a sheet - a big watch-out anger signal. Beside him, Jock was trying to wriggle his hands up to signal to his wife. And there were other men whom she knew.

The women stood silently side by side on the shore, eyes and faces anguished for their captured men. The big grey horse whinnied and curvetted as the officer spurred it on to the narrow plank leading to the boat. It stood twitching uneasily in the middle of the boat, crowding the men back into the bow and the stern. The officer held him firm and tilted his cocked hat.

'Cast off!'

For the first time, the watchers could see the man's face, tanned deep brown, his mouth tightly pursed, dark grey eyes narrowed against the light. Jock's wife gasped.

'Ye know who that is?'

Mary shook her head.

'Setton. Setton, one of the Glen lot.' A member of the crowd gasped and turned to her friends. 'A bad lot, he's always been a baddie.'

'And he's now an officer? In the Navy?'

Her friend nodded agreement.

'He was a right bully when he was a lad.'

An old man in front of them turned and muttered,

'An' they say he's a gamester as well.'

'Runs in the family. Well, I'm for off.' And the first speaker turned to wriggle and shoulder her way through the throng.

'Didna ken he'd taken a commission,' murmured someone else to her retreating back. She only shrugged.

Only officers of the Royal Navy could command press gangs, and members of the small community could scarcely look at each other in stunned amazement that such a man whom they knew as a low-life bully could reach such a rank.

Setton of The Glen! Even from twenty miles away the people in the little fishing village of Sillery shuddered at the sound of his name and his deeds. As well as his own reputation and his family's bad name, his ancestors had been enthusiastic Jacobites, supporting the return of the Stuart Catholic King, not a popular idea on the east coast. Not only that, it was widely known that one of his great-grandfathers fought in the rebellion about a hundred years ago, trying to rouse Scotland against the union with England, and to get French help in doing so. Since then, Mary knew from local gossip, the Settons had lost no opportunity to fight against the English. This, they said, was to keep the Auld Alliance going, an ancient agreement from the thirteenth century, between the Scots and the French. Called the Friends of the French, its ostensible aim was to ensure good trading. But, as most guessed, there was a more sinister aspect, in linking Scotland with France, against England and the Union of the Crowns.

So why was this one in the British Navy's press gang, for a Navy headed by an Englishman, and why then would he be fighting against the French?

CHAPTER TWO

'Did you find out where they're off to?' Harry's mother was by the fireplace, stirring something in a pot. The smell of a simmering broth made Mary's mouth water. Maggie's usual response to an emergency was to start a meal. Now the kettle was singing, the fire crackling as cheerfully as if to welcome the man of the house coming back from his fishing trip. But this time, there was no returning hungry cold man to be welcomed. This time his grandmother sat by the hearth, her skirt spread back over her knees, her bony shins warming at the coal fire, and rocking herself, crooning, 'My Harry, Oh, my Harry.'

'Aye. The provost told me. Edinburgh. To Leith. Then on to London and on to a warship.' Mary sat down in the other fireside chair, too weary and saddened to lift her feet to take her boots off. Maggie bent down and unlaced the heavy boots, pulling them off, to let her daughter-in-law stretch and warm herself. Mary rubbed her shoulder under the torn dress. She would have mending to do tonight. She was exhausted and sore from the fight and struggles, trying not to weep and distress Maggie and old Grannie even more.

'Whit else did the provost say?' Maggie asked.

'Oh, something about needing men for the Navy because the French and Spanish are getting a big fleet together.'

'How does he ken all that?'

'He said word had come through to the Town Councils that the Frenchies were planning to invade us.'

'Invade Britain? Never!' Maggie was firm. 'The thing's impossible.'

Mary pulled up her skirts to warm more of her cold body.

'Broth, lassie?' Maggie handed her a steaming bowl and a spoon. 'Sit you there, by the fire.' She turned to fill another bowl for the old grandmother.

Mary supped greedily, the goodness of the soup warming her chilled heart as much as her cold body. She rubbed her aching shoulder again, and as she moved, her sleeve rustled. She remembered she had taken some paper when it had fallen from Setton's torn coat lining.

'Look at this!' She spread out the paper. 'Dinna ken what it is.'

'Where did you find this?' Maggie was curious. Mary chuckled.

'It fell out of the horseman's coat tails when I was being dragged along, and I clutched at the tails and hung on. The lining tore – and there was the paper.'

'Might be useful?' Maggie asked.

Mary grinned in reply and spread it on her knee, then looked up in dismay. Though she had enough schooling to read and write in English, most of these did not seem to be English words. She spelt one out loud.

'"E C O S S E",' she said, and another, '"R E G I M E N T". Well, that looks like English. But it's not making sense to me,' she told Maggie and Grannie. '"N A V I G U E R",' she went on, and, unable to stop, she spoke the next word: '"FRANCE".'

Maggie and Mary stared at each other.

'That … could be … could it be … spy stuff …' Maggie stumbled over the words. Mary nodded. 'Is he after spies? Or is he a spy himself? He was never a good man. He might come after you.'

'No, he's off on the boat.' Mary was sure. 'And look here.' She stretched out the other crumpled paper. At the top was the heading 'Exemption Certificate'. And beside this heading was a scrawl of '*For the Captain.*' But otherwise, the paper only contained headings such as 'Name', 'Reason for exemption', 'Signature'. It was signed, but she couldn't read the writing.

She read the printed matter out to Maggie and they looked at each other.

'Could this get Harry off the boat?' Maggie fingered the certificate gently.

'Worth a try!' Mary was keen. 'Looks like it's been signed but it's not very clear.'

She fingered the paper and the smell of the horse came with it. The memory of the officer's assault, the flanks of the animal pushing her back, struggling to keep her footing, terrified of falling under the horse's hooves, and clutching at the man's coat, his coat lining ripping – the fear and anger swelled again as the memories returned. She struggled to clear her feelings.

'What else can I do but try to get him off the ship?' she asked pitifully. 'I'd like to go after them … I'd like to be with Harry but … I cannae leave you, Mother Maggie. Not with old Grannie here needing help.'

'Aye, lass, we need you. But we need Harry too.' Maggie was twisting her apron again. 'Maybe try one thing at a time. Get that bit of paper to the ship's captain, maybe, and get Harry off.'

Mary looked at it. She was the only one in the household who could read so she had no help in understanding the paper.

'Looks like it needs a name … then maybe what's the reason he should get off … and then his home … and …' Her voice trailed off. 'I'm not sure, but if I put his name at the top, we can sort out other things later.' She thought she could argue that the paper had been snatched before it had been completed. It was worth a try, she thought.

She reached for the pen and ink which Maggie always kept handy on the mantelshelf, and with some purpose in her head now, she put Harry's name at the top of the Exemption Certificate.

Mary set off back for the ships at the quay. Find a captain, find someone who knows what to do, she thought. A certificate, an Exemption Certificate – surely that could get Harry off.

But all the men she saw shook their heads.

'Exemption Certificate? Canna help you

there, lass, that needs an official Navy ship's captain.'

Disappointed and defeated, she flinched and turned away.

'Mistress! Mistress Watson!' one skipper called her. She turned, hopeful once more. 'You'll have to go over to Leith to get to his captain.'

'If the ship hasna sailed ere this time,' someone else added. 'Or you might even have to chase it to London.'

'Aye,' said another, 'that's where the fleet's likely going to start from, then other ships maybe from other ports.'

'London!' She was aghast. 'That's … miles away!'

'Aye, sorry, lass, but the captain of the right ship has to see this paper.'

She turned away, horrorstruck. London was only a name to her, as a big fearsome place. No, she didn't want to go to London, but, but … she stumbled over her thoughts. Harry was off to London, and, therefore, would she go too?

That was quite a trip, and a big plan to be made. What to do?

CHAPTER THREE

Back home Mary told Maggie and old Grannie of the ideas.

'You're no …' Maggie Watson looked up in alarm. 'Mary, you can't. It's a long way to Leith. And even more to London.' Maggie had never been further than St Andrews, just round the coast. 'And London! It's not a place for a young woman by herself.'

'Aye. Aye. I'm wanting to go to Leith. I'm not letting them take Harry. Not without trying to get him back.'

Privately Mary thought Leith was the furthest she was likely to go. The thought of London horrified her. She had always been keen to travel – but by herself? More women even of her age now travelled by themselves these days, she knew, especially those who needed work. To find good employment sometimes they had to travel to 'situations' away from their homes. But she had never needed to do that, and though she was an adventurous young woman, there was still a degree of caution in her nature, making her wary of such a big adventure. She would be alone and unprotected. On the other hand, she thought, I'd be on a boat, and I'd be in an inn, so there would be people there to help.

Her thoughts went round and round until she was nearly dizzy. But Maggie had begun to speak again.

'Aye, well, there is that. Getting Harry back. But you havenae ever been far from home and you're a young lassie.'

But old Grannie Watson nodded.

'I'm old and I'm cold – otherwise I'd be there with you.'

'What … what will we do without you?' Maggie screwed up her face, trying to stem the tears over this new horror come upon her. 'Grannie needs you, I need you …' Her voice trailed off. She would have to look after old Grannie Watson, cook and clean, and do all the laundry, and the shopping for food. And there was the selling of fish – but there would be little fish to sell without the catch that Harry got them.

Mary was torn. She was needed here. But if she could get Harry back, then Harry and she would come straight home, and Maggie would get the support she needed. She was decided.

'I'm going to Leith, and let's hope the ships are still there.'

'What will you when you get there?'

Mary frowned.

'Try to get him off the ship. Speak to the Captain. Somehow.'

Grannie Watson was eyeing a jar on the mantelpiece.

'I have some savings here, lass. Go and get my grandson back.' Her voice was shrill and shaky, but determined, and Mary looked down on her with love and pity. Harry meant everything to the old woman. Since she'd lost her own husband and two oldest boys to the sea, she'd set her heart on Harry and his brother, Tom. Tom was in Aberdeen, working on what he called 'the big boats', going into deeper and deeper waters to try to catch bigger fish. Harry was content to stay in Fife, beside his mother and grandmother, and to set up house with his childhood sweetheart.

Even before they'd thought of love, they'd been friends, playing together round the streets. Fifteen and more years of knowing Harry wasn't going to disappear overnight, not if she could help it.

Maggie shook her head.

'I don't like it,' she said. 'I'm feared for you. And you've got that other wee bit o' paper as well. What's that all about?'

Mary sat down again beside her in the kitchen.

'Ma, we'll write to Tom before I go, and he can come back to be with you and Grannie here. You'll be grand.' Mary squeezed her hand and put an arm round Grannie.

'But what about you? That boat ride to Leith. And maybe,' Maggie could scarce bring herself to say it. 'Maybe, further on, and think about that – all that long way.'

'Folk do it all the time, Ma. Remember Jeannie Craddock? She went to be a housemaid in London to Lady Fraser, her that came here for a visit.'

'So she did,' said Maggie, remembering. 'She went on the stagecoach, and then wrote back to her folk that she was having a grand time. You had to read it to them.'

'An' there were others,' said Grannie, coming back from her nightmare. 'Bella, her from the next street, she went to Edinburgh and then on to London. Her mother told me.'

Maggie and Mary exchanged glances. Bella from the next street was not the example they would have chosen. Nonetheless, it was clear that young women could and did travel to faraway places, by themselves.

'If you go, lass, we'll need to help you.' Grannie was back to her strong self again. 'You must bring him home, lassie. We all have need of him. But how are you going to do the thing?'

'Grannie, I'll do my best, and I dinna rightly ken. Get to see him afore he gets on the ship, maybe.'

'What's the timing?''

'I'll get on Geordie's boat to Crail, then on to Leith.'

'Aye,' said old Grannie. 'Even Leith's a lang way. You'll need some silver.' And she pushed herself to her feet and drew down the jar from the mantel.

'Aye, you're right, old Grannie.' And Maggie too found some money, from a pot on the dresser.

Mary was aghast.

'I cannae take your silver!' she said.

'You must! You need to keep it safe, though.' Maggie told her. 'Put it in this pouch and hide it under your skirt, clipped into your waistband.'

Mary allowed Maggie to help her attach the pouch, carefully attaching it to her waistband and hiding it underneath the full skirt.

News of Mary's decision to get to Harry flew round Sillery like the seagulls round the fishing boats. The older men shook their heads as she passed them in the street later that day. The men leaning on the seawall nodded to her as she walked back.

'Dinna be glaikit! You're a young lassie, what can you do?'

Her anger at being called daft made her, unusually, shout at them.

'You go after them then,' she flashed back at them. 'You get the men off that boat.'

They drew on their pipes. Either they didn't hear her, or they didn't want to.

She found Geordie, the man who ran the boat to Crail, and asked him for a passage the next morning.

'We'll be off early, lass,' he said, giving her a careful look. 'I hear tell you're after your man, is that so?'

She nodded, and drew out the Exemption Certificate.

'Look,' she said, 'I've got this. Have you seen the like before? Do you think it'll work?'

Geordie took the crumpled paper and scanned the printed words, squinting at the signature at the bottom.

'You've put his name in – and maybe the others, too?'

'That's what I thought.'

Geordie was thoughtful.

'Aye, it might work, an' all. I doubt you'd need to give it to an officer, though.'

Mary thought of the Lieutenant who had commanded the press gang, and shivered.

'How would I know which officer?'

Geordie shrugged.

'You could ask the skipper, Geddes, when you're on the Leith boat. He might be able to tell you.'

Hope in her heart, Mary went into the one shop that Sillery boasted.

'So you're going after them?' Mistress Wood weighed out the flour and sugar, and poured them into bags. 'Not a good idea. Not for a young girl.'

'We've been sweethearts all our lives, Mistress.' Mary packed the bags into her basket and paid over the money. 'I can't let him go without trying to help.'

'What are you going to do if ... when ... you find him?'

'Mistress, I don't know. I don't know. Try to get him off the ship. I have to go and try.'

'I ken, lassie, I ken. He's your man.' Mrs Woods' tone changed from criticism to understanding.

Mary nodded and turned to the door.

'Mistress Mary, lass ...' Mistress Woods was at her side as she left the shop. 'Have you thought of, well, maybe if you canna get him off, had you thought of maybe going with him? Maybe being one of yon nursing women on the ship? You're grand at helping folk.'

'You mean ... on board a big ship?' Mary's main thought, the one she'd made public, was to get Harry off. But in fact there had been nigglings of other ideas, supposing he couldn't be released.

'Aye, lass, I ken it's not the usual thing for a lassie but well, you do a lot round here and maybe if you have to go further with Harry, there might be a fair few injuries if the men have to fight a battle. You might have to think of ... maybe a lot of blood, and ... well ... other things.' Mistress Wood stopped, and shook her head, 'Ach, never heed me, lass, I'm just one of these independent women. I've had to look after myself and the weans for a long time.' True, thought Mary, Mistress Woods had been left with the bairns and nothing but her own two hands. Work of any sort had been her answer to widowhood and poverty.

'Aye, I had sort of thought there might be something I could do,' Mary admitted. Not for worlds would she tell Mistress Wood that she had actually pictured herself on board a big ship, helping care for the wounded. Sometimes it was a fleeting dream, and other times it was a nightmare.

Mistress Wood drew back.

'Ach, lass, just bide at home. Grannie Watson needs you, and so does Mistress Maggie.'

Mary groaned inwardly. She owed her family a duty, too, as well as Harry's family. They lived in Anstruther, only a step or two away, and even though Mary had siblings, there might be help needed in Anstruther.

'All the same!' She was definite, and thinking hard. 'I want to be with Harry so it's no' a bad idea. Maybe it's something I could do.' She had helped a fair few folk in her time, starting as a lassie when her mother was sick, helping cool her temperature by wiping her face and neck, helping her take her medicines, and … she remembered too, helping her own grandmother get to bed, get up and helping her to walk. Even as a child she was the one who was asked to take care of the other children. But wiping noses, and foreheads and faces was very different to what she'd see on board ship. She had helped with fishermen's injuries, though, helping bind the wounds from careless movements, and fashioning a sling out of rags for broken wrists. So maybe she had some knowledge, after all, though minimal. Caring for sick and injured people was something she enjoyed. The locals knew that and would come for her if they wanted help. She tucked the idea of caring at the back of her mind, for later thought.

She left Mistress Woods, anxious and upset for her, and walked along the cobblestones home. There she found Jeannie Farquharson, Jock's wife.

'Mary, Mary, if you go … will you give Jock this from me?'

Mary took the ring.

'Aye …'

Jeannie's face was wet.

'And, and, and … give him … my love, please.'

Jeannie's sadness sounded like a farewell, like she'd given up any hope of Jock's return. For a moment Mary wondered too. Would the men get back somehow? And if so, how was it to be managed? Or was this the end for them all?

Mary hugged Jeannie hard and stood holding her close until Jeannie gave a sob and ran out of the house. Mary stood, looking after her, twisting the ring between her fingers. In one short morning, their lives had changed completely.

Mary moved into Harry's and her room. Harry's nightclothes lay under the pillow, his nightcap on the table beside the bed, and his best clothes were on the bed, ready to put away after their Sunday outing to the kirk. Was this a time to be impulsive, or to take care? She didn't know, but her overwhelming wish was to be near her husband, to follow him, to help if she could. And Geordie who ran the Crail boat had said he could get her on the boat to Leith the next day. So she had to pack some clothes.

Blinking back her tears, she opened the kist and took out a roll of canvas. What would she need? Clean hose and a clean shift, mittens for the cold, a spare shawl, too. A cloth that would do as a towel, toothpowder and soap. She thought of taking her Sunday clothes, but instead added her best petticoat in case she needed to change. She checked at her throat: the little charm Harry had given her when they were children, on its ribbon, was there as it always was. She rolled the canvas neatly and bound it. The pack full, the bed bare: one thing left, she thought – the piece of paper. She drew it out. The dried bloodstains streaked across the surface, almost hiding some letters. She turned it over and looked again, more closely this time. Was that a list of names? Setton, Campbell, Cleary … and on went the list. Maybe about twelve in all, she thought, though she couldn't read all of them.

Thinking hard, she twisted it round further, turned it upside down, as if that would help clarify the letters. Was it possible that this was a list of – what? Conspirators? And Setton had it? What was it, what did it mean? This little fishing village in Scotland with a green glen inland – there could be no connection with anyone important, surely, she thought. But … she wondered. Should she take it to the Provost? Maybe she should take it to someone in Edinburgh. Or might she get into trouble if it was known she'd taken the piece of paper, and if she was in trouble she might not be able to get after Harry in time to rescue him.

She fingered the paper again, turned it over, then folded it into a small square. Decision time! It might be useful to her. She'd wait to see what happened. Maybe, if that officer wanted it back, if it was precious to him, maybe she could use it as a bargaining tool – You want your paper, Lieutenant?

Give me Harry! She tucked it into her skirt pocket with her coins, checked the straps on her pack, and moved back into the kitchen.

Maggie was standing at the mantelpiece, shifting the bits and pieces along the mantelpiece, the candlesticks, the Bible, a couple of pretty shells, sliding them, lifting them, caressing them. She turned to Mary.

'He made me this.' Maggie fingered a tiny roughly carved wooden shape. 'A bonnie wee terrier. He said,' and she pressed it to her mouth, 'it was like the dog we used to have when he was a wee boy. Oh, Harry, Harry, my son, my son. Where are you now?'

Mary went over to her mother-in-law and put her arms round her. She held the older woman's shaking body for what seemed a very long time, until Maggie moved away.

'I'm not going to cry any more,' she said firmly, wiping her face. 'I had to have a wee weep.'

'Mmm,' came from the chair by the fireside. Mary and Maggie turned and looked down at Grannie Watson. Her face was chalk white, her hands held out to the fire, her skirt turned back over her knees. She was rocking back and forwards, intoning 'Mmm mmm mmm mmm.'

'What is it, old Grannie?' asked Mary gently.

'Mmm mmm mmm mmm. Mmm Harry... ha ha harry. Tammas, Jock, they're all gone. They're all gone.' She was staring as if into another world, seeing the ghosts of her menfolk, who had left her to struggle into old age, with no man to warm her bed, no son to laugh at her foibles and remind her of her own youth with memories of his childhood. And now no grandson to light her life.

Her grief was almost tangible, forming a glass bubble between her and the world.

'Harry's mother, I can't leave you with this,' Mary whispered.

'Aye, aye, lass, we'll be all right. You must find Harry for us all.'

'I'll be ready to go at first light. I'm all packed.'

Maggie sighed.

'Do you think you'll be able to get Harry off the ship?'

'Dinna ken, as yet. Geordie says I'll have to show that Certificate to an officer. He says maybe the skipper, Geddes, will know, on the Leith boat. He'll maybe tell me to speak to the Captain of Harry's ship.'

'And if that doesnae work?' Maggie enquired.

'I was going to try to speak to Harry, tell him we're feart for him, and ... that we tried.' She looked pleadingly at her mother-in-law. 'Maybe even just to see him ...'

'And then, you'll be back?'

'Aye ... aye ... I think so. Hope so.' Mary straightened up. 'We'll both be back!'

Grannie reached out a hand to her.

'If you can't get Harry off, what will you do?'

'Mistress Woods,' Mary began slowly, 'said that maybe I could nurse ... on the ship.'

'Mercy!' Grannie pressed her hands to her mouth. 'You canna go. You canna. You're over young, a bit lassie.'

'Aye, she's in the right of it,' Maggie agreed with Grannie. 'It's no safe. That's what it's no. Harry wouldna want you to be feart and ... maybe ... have problems.' She didn't want to specify what kind of problems. But Mary could guess.

'I have to go.' Mary was half pleading, half trying to convince herself. To nurse, on the ships, was maybe the one way she could be with Harry, if he was stuck on the ship.

Maggie nodded, seeing that Mary's mind was not made up.

'Aye, I ken. Harry and you belong together. You'll maybe have to try.' She made no mention of being left alone, to nurse Grannie, to bring in some fish, collecting the fish off the sea wall where the tide hurled them, filleting them, selling them to bring in some money.

But Mary understood.

CHAPTER FOUR

Next morning found Mary on the shore early. Geordie, the Crail ferryman, had his boat ready and waiting to take her to the link up with the Leith boat. He handed her into his small boat. She settled as comfortably as she could in the prow, aware that she should keep out of his way as he and his mate pushed the boat out into the water, and picked up the oars. Once out into the deeps, Geordie would steer for Crail. It would take an hour maybe to reach the bigger boats at Crail which would be sailing to Leith.

The rhythm of the oars, the lap of the tide, the day's gentleness of the inshore waters soothed the tension created by the past hours: the anger and anxiety at the press gang work, Harry's face as he was captured, and the grimness of the trapped men on the boat. Also in her consciousness was the horror felt by the families, and the fears for the future, for their men, and for their own struggles to make a living. But the mere fact of setting off on the journey, with the major purpose of seeing Harry, finding out more, perhaps getting him released with the exemption paper which she'd discovered, helped fill her mind with new thoughts. This journey, perilous though it might be, thrilled her with the novelty of new worlds. And the gentleness of the waters lulled her tired mind.

'Ahoy!' Geordie's bellow roused her from her dreams. She blinked and stared about her. They had reached the Crail harbour, and there was the boat for Leith. She moved slowly, Geordie's hand helping her balance, and climbed the steep and slippery steps on to the quay. He went before her, reaching down a helping hand to steady her and pull her up the steps.

Once on the quay Geordie guided her over to the Leith boat.

'The skipper – there he is.' He caught the eye of the skipper and touched his cap, indicating a respectful wish to talk.

'Mr Geddes, this is Mistress Mary Watson, from Sillery. Her man wiz pressed, and she's wishful to find the ship they'll be usin' to get the men to London. And I'm making sure she gets to Leith to see if she can find her man.'

The skipper smiled, but his face was bleak, his mouth turned down.

'Welcome aboard, Mistress, any help we

can gie ye, we will.' He turned to Geordie. 'Aye, the press has been busy this week or more. We hae lost a few men.'

'I've this bit of paper,' said Mary, drawing out the exemption certificate. 'Do you think this would get him away?'

Skipper Geddes looked carefully at the paper, then at Mary. If he asked her how she had it, what would she say? But he seemed to be a cautious man.

'It might, and it might not. But you'd need to show it to the captain of the ship he's put on. I doubt it'll do no good till then. Come,' he said, and offered his arm. 'Let me take ye on to this boat, Mistress. We'll be in Leith ere night.'

She turned to thank Geordie but he'd hurried away. No pennies for him, he would refuse to take anything for helping her. What good men are the Fifers, thought Mary, as she walked along the quay.

'What is the cost of the voyage, sir?'

'Och, no.' The skipper frowned away the question. 'We are put on this earth to help each other, are we no? And I would help any lassie in this case. The gang is wicked, taking our fishermen like that.' He helped her on board, and they soon set off.

Leith at last! Mary was glad to get on shore.

'This way, Mistress.' The skipper was guiding her along the quay. But there were no naval ships tied up there, nor could she see any bigger ships out on the Firth. Only trading vessels came and went and sat at anchor. The skipper was shading his eyes, searching the horizon, and looking all round.

'Maybe we have missed them, Mistress.'

She bit her lip. She'd been counting on finding Harry here, counting on Geddes to hand the Exemption Certificate to the ship's captain, relying on that to get him off the ship. She'd set her sights too high. There were no ships that either Geddes or she could see. The certificate, clutched in her hand, seemed useless.

'We'll walk further, Mistress, and ask.'

They set off. Further along the quay, by the round house, her attention was hooked by none other than Lieutenant Setton himself.

What?! Setton here? Did that mean that the ships were here somewhere, the ship to which Harry had been taken? Maybe she could get to him, get to the ship, get him off?

'Skipper! Look! There's Lieutenant Setton, who commanded the press gang. He's here! Does that mean the ships are here?'

'Maybe, maybe. Bide here.'

He left her standing on the quay by his own ship, while he strode off to where Setton was standing, arguing, it looked like, with someone else. The skipper passed by the pair without so much as a sideways glance, but Mary was sure he had noted the argument.

Setton glanced up, and saw her. He made a sudden movement as if he would hasten to her, and she stepped nearer to the Crail boat, as if it could be a refuge. His eyes were fixed on the paper in her hand. He abandoned his argument, and moved towards her purposefully. Mary clutched the certificate more tightly to her bosom. No way would she give that up. Rather she would scream and fight.

With a gasp of relief she saw the skipper stride past Setton, ignoring him, and moving fast towards her. He was shaking his head. Meaning, she thought, that Harry's ship had set sail.

Lieutenant Setton hesitated as the skipper passed him. It was a large quay, but Setton sped up and maybe would reach her before the skipper got back to her. And then he would grab the paper. How could she avoid him? The skipper was moving faster too, and he pointed to his left. Oh, an inn! Would she have to stay the night here before she could return to

Sillery – or go further? She stepped over the cobblestones to meet Mr Geddes at the inn door.

He was somewhat breathless.

'I fear, Mistress, we seem to be too late here. You must go on to London. There'll be a boat in the morning that'll take you there – the innkeeper here will know.' As she hesitated at the inn door, Mr Geddes went on. 'I wish I could go with you, but I have my own duties. But, my advice, lass, is first of all, put that paper away.' He lowered his voice. 'An' mind that fellow there.' He indicated the hovering Setton, unable to get near them. 'He might look like a gentleman, but I doubt he's to be trusted. But the innkeeper here is a good man,' he continued. 'You can trust Bob Stott. And a few others,' he added, nodding at a gentleman who was approaching the inn as if they might be acquainted. And indeed as he stood back to let the gentleman go into the inn before them, he put out a hand and spoke in a low, confidential voice. 'Can I trouble you for your kindness to my young friend, here, sir, for she might have to travel on to London and I daresay you might be going in the same direction.'

The man raised his eyebrows, and bowed politely to Mary.

'Certainly, Skipper.' His dark hair, straight profile and fine blue coat tugged at her memory. Surely she had seen him before? She turned to the skipper, meaning to ask the man's name, but he was on the move.

'Good luck, Mistress! God go with ye.'

'I canna thank ye enough!' Mary called after him.

She turned back to the inn, but already the gentleman was waving her inside. Her heart jumped as she suddenly remembered where she had seen him before. He was the one who had been at Sillery – his was the hand, she was sure, that had grabbed and torn off a bit of the paper she carried.

But before she could do or say anything, a man came out of a back room to meet them, his scanty hair lifting in the breeze from the door.

'I'm Bob Stott, the innkeeper. Are you wanting a room?' He rubbed his hands on his apron.

'If you please, yes, thank you, Mr Stott, I would like a single room.'

'Just follow me. By yourself, are you?' He picked up her pack.

Mary nodded.

'Yes, yes ... for the moment. I'm going to see my husband.'

'And where might he be?' demanded Bob Stott, pushing open the door into a timbered hallway.

The smell of food tickled her nostrils and she caught her breath. When had she last eaten a good meal?

'In the Navy. I'm wanting to say Godspeed.'

'Leaving you behind, like?'

Not likely, was Mary's first thought, but she smiled and nodded.

'Aye, Mistress, this war with Bonaparte has gone on long enough. We lost our boy. At least, he was pressed last month, and we haven't heard a thing since then.'

Mary froze with horror. Was this to be Harry's and her fate too?

'I'm so sorry.' She found her voice trembling. 'I thought they only took seamen.'

'Aye, the laddie was keen to go to sea, he was doon by the shore, watchin' the ships. Maybe they thought he was a seaman.'

Mary repeated,

'I'm sorry!'

'Aye, thank ye, the wife feels it terribly. So do I.'

She followed the landlord through a doorway at the back of the hall, and up a narrow staircase. The steps were rough but there was a good banister to hold on to. At the top was a short passageway, lit only by one sputtering lamp. He opened the first door on the left.

'In here, Mistress, if you will.'

Mary surveyed the small room, single bed with smooth bedclothes, bedside candle, and chair. Knobs for her clothes to hang on. A tiny dresser with a washbasin and jug. Mr Stott hovered by the door.

'You came off the Fife Packet, did you no? Sam Geddes' boat?'

'Aye, I did. He said he knew you?'

'Aye, aye, that's right. A good man. You're a friend of his?'

'I am,' said Mary firmly.

'You let me and my wife know what you might need, Mistress, and maybe we can help.' She nodded her thanks. 'I'll leave you be now, you come down in half an hour and I'll get you a warm posset. Maybe you'll be wanting supper?'

She nodded enthusiastically at the sound of supper, and he smiled as he closed the door.

CHAPTER FIVE

Left to herself she spread out the contents of her pack on the bed. One creased shawl, clean shift and stockings, her hairbrush, towel and soap. She hung her shawl and cloak on the hooks on the wall. Her clean clothes she spread out in the kist at the foot of the bed, and toothpowder and soap lay beside the jug and bowl. Unpacking completed, she sat down on the bed and pulled off her half boots, wriggling her toes in relief. Then she removed the crumpled papers from her pocket and stood for a moment, smoothing them out. She still could not understand the scrawl on the larger piece, but instinctively she felt it to be important. The small window gave little light to help her. She lit the candle and held it to the paper. She peered again in the better light. No luck. There seemed to be more words scrawled across the scrap, torn off at the edge, but she could not distinguish them in the poor light.

She pushed them into her bodice for safety,

and tucked them in, out of sight.

She poured cold water from the jug into the big blue bowl on the dresser, and washed her face and hands. The black-spotted mirror swung forward and showed an enlarged face – pale, black shadows under the eyes, dark hair tousled.

A sound outside the window startled her. She peered out on to the broad Leith street, wondering what she would see. The noise of the docks had diminished as evening came, and this was only a couple of men stumbling along the greasy cobblestones. Dear goodness, what was this she had got herself into when two drunk men would make her jump. A thought for the old days of safety, as near as last week, brought tears to her eyes. Tight-lipped, she forced them back and pulled her brush through her hair. She twisted it up into its combs, settled her shawl round her shoulders. A quick glance in the mirror showed her to be as neat and tidy as could be expected. She smoothed out her skirt, locked her door and descended towards the inn's dining room. She was cold, colder than she should be, with the warmth of the inn in every room.

The landlord was waiting for her.

'Come you in here, Mistress.' He opened the door to a small room opposite the dining room.

'This is what we keep for, eh, lone

travellers.'

She walked slowly into the small room and stood for a moment at the door. From there she could see into the dining room across the passage, with a number of tables inside, people eating and talking. Beyond them, by the steamed-up window, a man sat at a table on his own with his back to her, broad shouldered, in a coat of dark blue cloth. His head was turned from her, staring out the window, but even so, she thought, he looked familiar. But, as she told herself, so many men wore this uniform of dark blue. Turning back to the little room she had been shown, she sat down at the table near the fire, where an older woman was setting out a bowl of steaming soup and a slice of bread.

'Will you have ale, Mistress?'

Mary shook her head. All she wanted was the soup and bread and maybe a sup of tea. She sipped her first course of soup, aware of the silence in the other room where the men had downed their ale, and were now surreptitiously staring at her.

'I'm Annie, Mistress, I'll be looking after ye.' She ladled yet more soup into Mary's dish and as Mary looked up to thank her, she saw the man at the window get up, and pick up his gloves from the table. As he half turned to move towards the door, she had a clear view of his profile. It certainly was the officer in charge of the press gang. It *was*

Lieutenant Setton! Again! Surely, he would have sailed off with the press gang he led. Or had the pressed men gone ahead, leaving the press gang here to gather more 'volunteers'? Or was he on his own? Setton looked to be by himself, at least in the inn. He turned, and she looked down hastily, stooping, ostensibly to pick up her dropped napkin. When she sat upright again, he had gone. The men at the centre table shuffled their chairs back noisily and also moved out of the dining room.

Alone in the small room, she nibbled at the chicken which had followed the soup. Delicious! But her mind was on bigger things. Could she have missed the naval ships in the dock? If Setton was still here, was there a chance she might still catch Harry here in Leith? If Lieutenant Setton had been a different man, she might even have had the courage to ask him – but there was something about him, she thought, shivering at the memory of how he strode across the harbour towards her earlier. It wouldn't hurt to be very careful, she thought.

Mary wiped her mouth with the napkin she had dropped.

'Is there a back stair to my room?' she asked, hesitantly. Annie looked sidelong at her.

'Are ye wanting to stay away from the boozy men?'

Mary nodded.

'Aye, Mistress, I'll show ye. Come you this way,' Annie touched her arm. 'It's the one we servant lassies use ourselves.' She showed Mary a small twisting stairway at the back of the tavern. 'It will lead up to your room.'

Mary picked up her skirts and climbed up, pressing against the close walls. At the top she paused, trying to get her bearings. She clutched her room key in her hand and cast a quick glance along the corridor. Her eyes narrowed as she spotted a man coming out of a room at the far end. Surely that was *her* room? Surely … that was Lieutenant Setton? Nervous and remembering his fierce glare, she sidled along the corridor, hugging the wall and hiding behind a pillar, but in a moment the officer was away, down the main stairs and out of sight. Unnoticed, she reached her doorway. She had been right, it was her room she had seen him leave. Without thinking she flung open the door. There was no one inside, thank goodness, or she didn't know what she would have done. Shouted for help? Run to the landlord, she supposed.

She jumped as she noticed another figure standing beside a different door, trying to unlock it. He gave her a quick glance, and she recognised him – the gentleman that Skipper Geddes had asked to protect her.

'It seems this lock does not work, Mistress, I must ask the landlord.'

He was a well-looking man, with a blue coat and light breeches. Like Setton, but not the uniform blue which Setton wore. She acknowledged his comment with a slight curtsey and inclination of the head, and pushed her way into her own room. As she shut the door, she heard Mr Stott the landlord coming along.

'Oh Mr Cameron, this won't do. Let me help.'

Definitely not Setton, definitely known to the landlord. She wondered whether she should tell Mr Stott of her suspicions, but the murmur of voices and the slam of a door suggested that Mr Stott was busy and involved.

She shut her own door and turned the key in the lock. The mechanism was old, and it was a frail barrier, but would hold the door sufficiently to allow time for a scream or two if someone came in. Then she moved round the small room checking to see whether anything had been taken. Nothing had, but certain things had been moved slightly. Her hairbrush was not straight, and her cloak that she'd hung up was carelessly half off the hook – but then he could not have had long to hunt. What could he have been looking for?

It could only be the papers, surely. There hadn't been any reason to hide them, as far as she knew, but instinctively she'd tucked them away and kept them on her person. Now she pulled them out of her bodice and spread them out on the bed.

There came a sound outside and she started up towards the door. The chair would only hold it for a minute or two. What else could she pile against the door? The washstand perhaps? She tugged at it, but it refused to move. The bed itself? That was a fixture too. There was the kist at the foot of the bed, that would work. Gritting her teeth, she pulled the heavy chest over to the door, and jammed it hard against the thin wood. The noise had gone, there was no one there, she was sure. But she was also sure that no one would be able to enter her room, now.

Panting with the effort, she returned to the bed to examine the larger paper in more detail. She held the candle as close as she could. One or two letters began to form words as she tried again to read. 'Ordres' – that must be 'orders' in French, she thought. 'Il faut' – what was that? And at the end of the words there seemed to be a list of names, spilling off the end of the paper, torn off halfway during the scuffle in Sillery – the list that Geordie had seen.

What could it mean? she wondered. There was no denying that a note in French was suspicious. And to have it hidden in his coat lining. And then to search her room for it.

And that gentleman, Cameron – he had tried to seize the papers, too. Was he trying to pick them up to return them to Lieutenant Setton? Or had he an interest in them?

She loosed her hair and pushed it back. Time to sleep if she wanted to try and find Harry in the morning. And she could sleep now, she thought, with the door barricaded. Oh, she was missing Harry! She loved him and trusted him and leaned on him to help her. But now she was on her own, alone, and who could she trust?

Edinburgh was the capital of Scotland. Surely there were folk here she could trust? But she remembered some comments her father had made when she was growing up. Scotland and France, aye, the Auld Alliance, he'd said. We've got something going between us. Maybe there was still something, she thought, maybe there were French supporters in Edinburgh. Just supposing, Mary thought, trying to organise her ideas, that Setton was linked up with France. The bit of paper she'd carried off had French words in it. What was it doing in Setton's coat lining? She tried to remember all her father had said about the alliance between France and Scotland, so long ago. It was to try to prevent English invasions of both countries. But surely there was no need for that now? The Scots and the English were friendly, and they wanted to make sure the French didn't invade the British Isles. So any communication with France could be … treacherous, she thought.

CHAPTER SIX

Mary woke dazedly to an early morning clatter of people in the passageway going about their business. A quick glance at the chest against the door told her that it hadn't moved an inch. That was good, she thought, no one had tried to come in at night. Maybe she was becoming too suspicious. She got out of bed and moved the chest so that any chambermaid bringing up water for washing could get in easily.

She was just in time. As she swung her feet back into bed a knock came at the door and it opened.

'It's six in the morning, Mistress. Water, Mistress, water for washing.' This was a luxury indeed, Mary thought.

'Thank you.' She watched as the girl replaced the old jug with the new one she was carrying.

'Will you be coming down to breakfast, Mistress?' asked the maidservant.

'Yes, surely, in a short while.'

'Because make it a wee bit later – there's been a real stoushie here this morning,' the young woman confided.

Mary's curiosity was roused.

'A stoushie? I didna hear a thing.'

'Well, Mistress, some of the soldiers from the Castle cam' down to the docks here, and they were carousin' and the noise was something dreadful. And,' the girl leaned forward to within inches of Mary's ear, 'see, there's a press gang that's goin' up and down the coast, getting' oor men on to the big ships here in Leith. And the soldiers picked a fight with the sailors, an' one o' our folks here, that stays with us often, was hurtit in the shoulder. He hid his airm pit in a sling.'

All this was definitely of interest to Mary. She'd been told the ships with the pressed men had gone, but apparently this was not the case. She swung her feet out of bed again. Ships, here, at Leith. Harry. Jock. She'd go and find them.

Breakfast was quick, with the maids rushing to and fro. Mary peered curiously at the few breakfasters she could see across the passage, but nowhere could she see anyone resembling Lieutenant Setton.

Good, she thought, I'll get to the docks and find the ship.

'Mr Stott!' she called, moving into the hallway. 'Landlord!'

He came out of the kitchen door, rubbing his hands on a big apron.

'I want to try and find my husband's ship. Could you please tell me how?'

He eyed her narrowly.

'He wouldn't be one of the pressed men, would he? We were hearing about the press gang last night.'

She looked down.

'Yes, yes, he was pressed. From Fife.'

'In that case, Mistress, I'll go with you myself. I've got a bit of an interest in this. As you know. You'll need your room for another night, I'm thinking.'

She agreed, with a thought for her slender purse, and went to her room to get her shawl. She could feel the folded papers snug in her bodice. It didn't matter who looked in her room, among her things. If what he was looking for was the bit of paper, well, she had it safe.

'Mistress! Over here!'

Mr Stott, the landlord, was already waiting outside the inn's door. With a shy gesture he pushed back a flopping lock of hair on to his balding crown.

'Where do we go?'

'This way,' he said, waving an arm, and they began to walk. 'Ye needn't worry about money, Mistress, we won't charge you for another night. Seein' as your man was pressed. We like to help where we can.'

The noise of the docks had started up again at first light, and grew louder as they strode along the Shore. Hammers were clanging, food carts were rumbling alongside the boats to unload their goods. Men were unloading crates, throwing boxes on to boats, and yelling to each other. And groups of men were hurrying along the wharf and the jetty between east and west piers, to the small boats, ready to be rowed out to the big warships anchored offshore.

At the docks themselves there were small boats lined up behind others, bobbing in the water, bumping each other, with men balancing carefully trying to add more kists into the already loaded vessels. Mary could only walk carefully along the dock from one boat to the other, amongst a crowd of people seemingly intent on the same thing. The cobblestones were slippery under her feet, her movements ungainly, but despite staggering, she was determined to continue the length of the quayside. She stared at each boat as she stumbled towards it, only half-aware of Bob Stott at her side. Sometimes she thought she saw Harry, only to be disappointed. Once she was sure she saw Lieutenant Setton. She pulled her shawl closer and clenched her fists, cold in her woolly mittens. But it was someone else.

Aha! But there! Surely, surely that was Harry! She stared hard across the crowded jetty at the marching group. Was it him? She could only see the top of a reddish-haired crown. Looked like a stocky build, but she couldn't be sure. A red haired, maybe stocky man in the forefront of a hurrying group? She ran as fast as she could on the slippery spray-drenched cobblestones to catch up with the men. It looked like his back, the way he moved, his broad shoulders. Surely it was Harry!

'Harry! Harry!' She was so sure it was him: her voice was loud and excited.

The man turned his head. She took a step back in bitter disappointment. It wasn't Harry. But maybe someone would tell Harry that she was calling for him. What a dream! Maybe she could allow some hope? She couldn't bear to think of him, a free spirit, a gentle man, shackled, held down, forced into war.

The crowd pushed round her, as eager as she to look for men or to get to the ships. She struggled to keep her footing on the cobblestones. Bob Stott came up beside her, shading his eyes.

'Nae sign of my wee bloke, of course,' he said. 'Maybe if you find your lad you can ask after mine. I'll keep my ears open for any mention of your man. Give me his name and we'll do a deal. My boy was … is,' he stumbled over the words, 'Archibald Stott, Archie,' and he rubbed his eyes. 'And he was … IS … eighteen.'

Mary gulped. Eighteen! At the beginning of manhood.

'My man is Harry Watson, from Sillery in Fife.'

Many of the smaller boats were loaded. Men were rushing along the dock, casting off the big ropes, throwing them up to sailors on deck. She gazed up at the riggings. The sails were furled. The painted sides looked fresh. One by one, the ships were guided out of the harbour, then let go to make their way to the big warships.

'They're off. Off to London,' Mary overheard someone say. 'And then off to battle!'

'Aye,' someone else replied. 'It's our men that'll be fighting the Frenchies. And the Spanish. And us that has to bide at hame, and work. It's the women and bairns that suffer.'

'We'd suffer mair if the Frenchies invaded,' another woman said.

'Hope they come back!' That came from a number of the women.

Mary rubbed her eyes. She *would not* cry. Harry might just see her.

But Harry, if he was on any of these ships, would be below decks, and now be moving away, down to London to join the fleet. She was too inexperienced to tell a ship of the line from a frigate, or from a barque. But she did know that even here she was seeing a group of larger ships than she'd ever seen before. And that Harry was now far from seeing her, and she … far from seeing him. Tears stung in her eyes and rolled down her cheeks. She had been so sure she'd catch Harry in Leith. It was all for nothing. She hadn't seen him; he hadn't seen her, or known she was following, though he could guess how anxious she would be.

Bitterly disappointed, she slumped against a cask at the water's edge. Mr Stott was standing some way back from the crowd, talking to the that gentleman with the dark hair, the one who had appeared in the corridor last night. She'd heard Mr Stott call him Mr Cameron. Mr Cameron had removed his hat, and she noticed the man's hair streaked with red, glinting in the sunshine. He wore the dark blue coat which she remembered from yesterday, with blue breeches and shiny black boots. But this time, though, his left arm was in a sling. Could he have been the man whom the maid had mentioned, injured in the fight between the soldiers and the press gang? He looked fit enough, she thought, even with a bad arm. And she wondered at such an intense conversation. Was it about Archie? Could it, possibly, be about Harry and the pressed men from Fife?

In a few minutes Mr Stott was back beside her.

'I just stepped away for a word with Mr Cameron, Mistress, he bides with us when he's here. A very knowledgeable man about ships and the press, he is. He says they're off to London, indeed, Mistress. I doubt you'll find your man, unless you go to London.'

'London! London! That's away, so far, far, away down south in England.'

'Always has been, Mistress.'

What a journey, she thought to herself. Dare she go? Try it?

If I don't go…

They walked back to the inn silently. Mr

Stott seemed as disappointed as she – how often did he come here to look for his boy?

'It's a bad business, Mistress,' Stott said. 'But maybe if you go on looking for your man, maybe … might you come across our boy?'

She tried to focus on what Bob Stott was saying.

'Look for your boy too?' It seemed a big request.

He nodded.

'Just maybe to keep an eye open for him, Mistress. We'll tell you what he looks like.'

There was so much in her mind, so many thoughts spilling over. When she'd mentioned the possibility of London to Maggie and old Grannie, she hadn't really been serious, she thought, it was a vague, faint idea. But if she didn't go, then Harry was bound for five years. Or at least that was what she remembered hearing about pressed men's time of service. Harry, and Jock, and Mr Stott's son Archie, too. Five years! A lot could happen in that time. Harry might come back injured – or he might be killed in battle.

And what was she to do to help Maggie and old Grannie, let alone looking after herself?

CHAPTER SEVEN

Mrs Stott was standing at the door as they returned, hope in her eyes until Mr Stott shook his head. Please God, thought Mary, we will succeed. I will go to London. She had made up her mind.

'No word, yet,' said Bob Stott to his wife. 'Mr Cameron is on the lookout, but Mistress Watson here will keep her eyes out for him too. There's a lot of folk keeping watch for us, Chrissie my darlin'.'

Mr Cameron must not have been far behind them.

'Mistress Stott, indeed I will keep my eyes and ears open and do my best for you.'

'Thank you.' Chrissie Stott wiped her eyes on her sleeve and turned away, mouth down.

Mr Stott turned to Mary, and said, 'Mr Cameron, sir, can I present to you Mistress Watson from Fife? Mistress Watson, Mr Cameron is a very wise man in the ways of ships and the pressed men.'

Mary and Mr Cameron eyed each other carefully as he bowed and she curtseyed low.

'I take it from Bob here that your husband was pressed, Mistress?'

'Aye, indeed sir, that he was. Harry Watson from Sillery in Fife, with a few others too.'

'They'll be off to London shortly, Mistress: if you want to carry on your chase, it's there you'll have to go. If it helps, I'm heading that way myself by stagecoach, and I'm well accustomed to the road.'

'Thank you, sir,' was all Mary could think to say.

'Harry Watson – I'll remember the name, Mistress. There may be hope of releasing him, but I have to say it is doubtful. Sorry, Bob, but it's true.'

He bowed, a regretful look on his face, and walked back along towards the Shore. Mr Stott's shoulders slumped, but Mrs Stott reappeared from the inn.

'Come into the kitchen, Mistress, and have a drop of tea.'

Mary followed the Stotts into the timbered kitchen. Two women were washing up the mound of breakfast dishes, and there was a subdued clatter of plates being washed, dried and put away. The white painted walls were smoke-stained by the stove, and clear white by the door. She loved the homeliness of it, the warmth, the feeling of familiarity and belonging. The cosiness and intimacy prompted her to ask.

'Would I have seen someone coming out of my room last night after dinner? I was sure I saw a man there as I climbed up the last stair.'

Mr Stott's eyes narrowed.

'What like of a man?'

'I think his name is Lieutenant Setton.'

'Aha, Lieutenant Setton,' he said softly. 'What do you think he – if it was him – would want in your room?

She didn't answer directly.

'My things had been disturbed – moved about. I thought I caught a glimpse of him. If it wasn't him, it was someone very like.'

Mrs Stott opened her mouth, but Mr Stott held up his hand. She subsided.

'Maybe so, maybe so,' he said cautiously. 'But my question is still: what would he want in your room?'

Mrs Stott couldn't keep silent any longer.

'It's not as if you've got any great money on display. You're not wearing big jewels.'

Mary giggled.

'Mistress, if you could see our wee house in Sillery. Jewels is the last thing I'd be wanting. Rather I'd have big warm curtains!'

Mrs Stott laughed, the first lighter, happier sound Mary had heard from her. It eased the tension in the room. She poured out a cup of tea and Mary sat down by the big deal table, and sipped the hot liquid gratefully.

'Have you had dealings with him before?' asked Mr Stott. 'For you seem to me a respectable lass.'

'I am!' cried Mary. 'I've only seen him when he led the press gang that took my Harry. Then and yesterday, he was at the harbour when I arrived. I don't know him at all!'

'He must think you're of some use to him,' said Mr Stott. 'If you don't know him, then maybe you saw something? Or he thinks you saw something?'

What was he guessing? Did he know anything? She wondered. Her instincts were to trust this man and his wife – Skipper Geddes seemed to think she could – but she was afraid to talk of the papers, even of the Exemption Certificate. Any knowledge of that might hurt these two further. Could they have got one for their son? Maybe she should tell them. But she was nervous, and she didn't even know if the one she had would work. And maybe Mr Cameron who knew so much would have told him anyway. Mr Stott seemed to be quite friendly with Mr Cameron, and maybe because of this, Mary was inclined to be friendly towards Mr Cameron. But she had not yet made up her mind that either the landlord or Mr Cameron was safe to confide in.

So, silence on the papers, she thought.

'That would be unco' strange,' she said carefully, conscious of the papers tucked into her bodice. Mr Stott looked at her and mused,

'Aye, but there must have some reason for Lieutenant Setton to search your room. He shouldna have done that.' But his mind was elsewhere: he moved on to the press gang again. 'Aye, it's a bad business, a bad business. Men taken frae their families, never heeding what's needed to keep them, to work, to till the land, do the fishin'. A bad business. But we have to keep the Frenchies oot o' the country.'

'What's to do?' said Mrs Stott. 'We just have to keep on keeping on, and hoping. Like yourself.'

Mary set her cup down.

'I'd be pleased to have some advice. Should

I go to London? I could try to get on a ship, maybe as a nurse.'

'Well!!' Mr Stott sat back heavily in his big chair. 'You really want to follow him?'

'Aye,' she agreed. 'If I only see him, maybe …' Again, she was about to mention the Exemption Certificate but she held back. 'Maybe I can get on to the same ship, maybe as nursing assistant, or cook, or kitchenhand, something like that.'

Mrs Stott smoothed her clean apron and took up a stand by the fire, rubbing her hands at the blaze.

'That could be dangerous. It's not for decent women, being on board a ship like that. Looking the way you do, too. Maybe you should be disguised as a man? Cut your hair shorter, like.'

Mary put her hands to her glossy dark hair, braided thickly round her head.

'I havena got that far in thinking what's best to do. Not yet anyway.'

But on the way back from the dock she had made up her mind. She had definitely decided that if she could not get Harry freed, she would try to follow him. She felt a shiver up and down her spine. This was an adventure like no other. There were no choices to the ending: you took what came to you.

And the advantages? On the ship, there was danger but togetherness. Without her on the ship, Harry was by himself. And on shore, she was alone without Harry. What a choice!

'Think about it. Might be a good idea, disguise you, you ken.' Mrs Stott picked up a piece of hose from the table, and half-heartedly began to darn it. 'This is Archie's … Oh, where is he now? We don't know.' Her voice broke and she sobbed into her hands. Mr Stott got up from his chair and began to poke hard at the fire. Mary could not stay still - she stood and hugged Mrs Stott hard. Only Mrs Stott's sobbing broke the silence. Mr Stott was warming his hands at the fire, holding them out, then rubbing them, as if he was rubbing the limbs of his boy, cold in the warship.

'It's a long, long story, the story of a battle and the story of a war. And many folk suffer,' he muttered. 'But the short of it is,' he paused, 'our boy's gone. So you see, Mistress, we'll help you all we can. Maybe if we help you, somebody will help Archie, and the others.'

Mary smiled her appreciation at Mr Stott. 'Thank you, thank you kindly,' she murmured. 'Just tell me what your boy looks like.'

'Aye, well, if he's still like he was, he'll have brown hair, brown eyes, my height,' said Bob. 'An' what I'll do is go along to the docks to see if I can get you on board here, maybe no with your man, but alongside, like.'

Mrs Stott dried her tears. She lifted the steaming kettle from the stove, and poured a couple more hot drinks. Food was the great standby in times of big emotions, thought Mary, just like at home.

'Somethin' more to eat? A bit scone, like?' She moved to the stove, and the smells were wonderful. 'Time to get crackin'.'

Mary went to her side.

'Can I help you, Mistress?'

'That you can. Stir this until it thickens. Then you can peel some tatties. Thank you.'

Mary settled easily, stirring the big pot. The two servants slid in and out of the kitchen, carrying towels, basins, jugs. They glanced at her wonderingly, questioning what a guest was doing in the kitchen, let alone helping cook. She scarcely noticed them. Her thoughts were with Harry, with the trip to London, and a possible disguise.

'Off you go.' Mary looked up, startled. Mrs Stott was talking to the maids. 'Customers will be waiting.' Mary grinned to herself. Chrissie sounded just like her mother-in-law in a hurry. She finished stirring the porridge, moving the pot back away from the heat to prevent it boiling over. She moved to the table and picked up a knife. What a mound of tatties! It was a busy inn, this, with lots of folk going in and out. She guessed the Stotts knew a lot more than they were telling. As she did. And maybe so did Mr Cameron. He and Mr Stott were friendly. And he was going on the coach to London, staying at different inns on the road, no doubt. Would he be as friendly with other innkeepers? What kind of gentleman travelled a lot through the countryside on a stagecoach? Were there no other vehicles? No horses? She was truly ignorant, this little fishwife from Fife, she considered. And she might be seeing ghoulies and ghosties where none existed. But Cameron did puzzle her.

CHAPTER EIGHT

An hour or so later, Mr Stott walked in and sat down at the table.

'Pass me a bowl, lass, fill it up full as you can.'

Mary filled up a bowl, and pushed the porridge pot back on to the hob. She sat down beside him, anxiously questioning.

'What's the news?' Mrs Stott demanded, as she stirred more porridge for her breakfasting customers.

He broke some bread and took a bite.

'I canna get you on another ship ... I've tried all the places I know.'

Mary bit her lip.

'How…when… can I get to London?'

'Well, there's the stagecoach. It'll leave from the White Hart in the Grassmarket in about an hour or two's time. And I doubt it's full. There'll be a seat for you.'

'Mind you,' Mrs Stott added to her husband's information, 'it'll take you three nights on the road. And you'll have to sleep at other inns.'

'Ah well, you needna worry about that. There's room at inns for stage passengers. Even though you might have to share a room, there'll be a bed for you.'

He offered his empty bowl for a refill.

'Take some more yourself, lass, you'll need to keep fit for the journey.'

She laughed at that. A bowl of porridge to keep her fit – fit for what, she wondered. The journey, the unexpected, adventures.

She nodded.

'Aye. That's it! I'll go on to London on the stage.' With Mr Stott's efforts, and with the good night's sleep and good food, Mary's flagging energy was revived and with it her eagerness for the venture.

'And Maister Cameron'll be with you,' said Mrs Stott comfortably. Mary drew in a deep breath. Mr Cameron, with his arm in a sling. She nodded, in pretence of acceptance of Mrs Stott's comforting words, but again, she felt that frisson of mystery that Mr Cameron seemed to bring with him. This was no ordinary journey to get from one place to another. Into the unknown, with only a stranger for comfort.

She rose from the table.

'I'd best go and get ready. Thank you, both, for your kindness.' She left the room swiftly and almost ran up to her room, unlocked it and, once inside, looked through the room for odds and ends left out of her pack. She bound up everything carefully, and checked again that the precious papers were carefully hidden in her bodice. She was ready now for the stagecoach. Mr Stott was to make sure she had a seat.

She stepped carefully down the back stairs, and smiling at Annie, put her pack by the door, ready to take.

'I must say farewell, Annie. And to Mrs Stott if she is available.'

Mrs Stott moved out of the kitchen into the front area.

'God go with you, Mistress, our thoughts and blessings on you.' Her cheeks were wet, her eyes full.

Mary hugged her and moved off quickly,

lest she too be overwhelmed by leave-taking. She was leaving the friendliness, warm-heartednesss and kindness to go – where? And find – what? A young woman on her own, without the protection of her husband or male family members. Young women did such travelling, she knew, to go to situations such as domestic service. So it was not unusual. But these women were met by their employers. She was on her own.

She lifted her chin, defiantly, and went to join Mr Stott for the walk to the Grassmarket to await the coach.

Edinburgh closed around her, cold and tall, as she and Mr Stott climbed the hill up from Leith. She lost track of the turns and twists they took, the views down broad streets, the steep cobbled lanes. At last they were outside an inn with the sign of the White Hart, and the stagecoach was already under preparation. But for the moment there was a much greater distraction, for there above them was the Castle. She saw it lit by sunshine, in all its glory. Magnificent, it stood tall, solid on the craggy rocks, robust in its well-built walls, and strong and safe with its battlements.

Beautiful, incredible – she'd heard about it, read a little about it, seen an engraving once – but nothing had prepared her for its impact. And again, she wished she could explore further, visit this place, touch the walls of the Castle.

Someone pushed past her, maybe even pushed her, and she forced her attention back to her immediate surroundings. The Grassmarket tenements overawed her – what must it be like to live in one of these? Noisy, crowded, over-crowded probably, and likely smelly. She thought wistfully of Sillery, quieter, open and fresh. Traders at one end of the street had stalls laden with goods. She could see foods, wooden furnishings, clothes, and paints. She could hear cattle lowing somewhere in the distance, horses whinnying, and she could certainly smell them. Over all was the noise of people bustling, hustling, talking, shouting their goods, arguing.

A flicker of a dark blue coat caught her eye. Mr Cameron? Or Lieutenant Setton? Was it? Surely he would still be in Leith, near the ships. She shrank away from Mr Stott, into the shadow of the White Hart Inn. Please God Lieutenant Setton hadn't seen her, she thought. She stared at the spot where she thought she had seen him.

'A busy street, is it not, Mistress?' said a voice from beside her in the shadows. She gasped and turned, and caught an impression of smartness and elegance. Mr Cameron was standing there, his dark hair ruffled by the breeze, his blue coat and light breeches immaculate in the sunshine, his boots shining.

'Sir! I do beg your pardon. I knew not that you were standing here.'

He waved her apology aside.

'No difficulty, Mistress. I slipped out of the door of the White Hart a few seconds ago.' He gestured to the doorway. 'A fine place, is it not? Where Robert Burns once came?'

'Indeed, sir, I had not known that. Burns' poems of course I am familiar with and love dearly.' That was not only true but it would emphasize that she was no unlettered fishwife, unable to read or write. But if she were unable to write, she might never have kept that dangerous piece of paper …

'Mistress, you look concerned,' said Mr Cameron. 'Can I be of assistance?'

'No, thank you, sir …' Mary glanced up at him, and then caught sight of a dark, familiar figure across the Grassmarket. If it had not been Setton before, it was now – and he seemed to be heading straight towards the White Hart. 'Although …'

Cameron turned, and looked to see what she had seen. In a moment he had a reassuring hand under her elbow.

'Then let us make sure you are quite comfortable in the coach, shall we?'

She nodded, and moved fast with him along the cobblestones to where the coach horses were pawing, surprisingly calm in these noisy squabblesome surroundings. Mr Stott was standing by the open door.

'In you go Mistress, and God go with you.' He handed up her pack to the coachman, and Mary settled into her corner seat, leaning as far back as she could, reluctant to look out the window lest she see Setton or – even worse – be seen by him.

A middle-aged lady sat in the other corner, and as she had expected, a third corner was quickly taken up by Mr Cameron, just removing his hat.

'It will be a fine morning for a drive, methinks.' And he turned to the other woman. 'Let us introduce ourselves since we will be travelling companions. My name is Cameron, and I am a public servant.'

The older woman smiled.

'I, sir, and mistress, am Mistress Scott, travelling to visit my daughter who is about to give birth.'

Mary blinked. Her turn. What could she say?

'Mistress Mary Watson, at your service, mistress.'

'Are you travelling to look for a position?' asked Mistress Scott.

'Yes, yes, ma'am that's just what I am doing,' Mary replied. Well, it was true, wasn't it? The position of rescuer, for Harry.

Unseen by both women, Mr Cameron nodded his agreement.

CHAPTER NINE

'Congratulations to your daughter, and to you also,' Mary murmured.

'It will take us three nights and four days,' Mistress Scott announced, before settling back in her corner. The coach moved off. A lump of tension in Mary's breast eased and she leaned back against the leather seat, snuggling with comfort into the corner of the coach, a rug at her feet. But here she was, on her way to London! The early afternoon sun was bright and the cloudless sky seemed to promise a good journey. She shivered, then smiled. Harry! My love, she spoke to him in her head, I'm on my way to you. We'll be together soon. Her eyelids drooped, long lashes shading soft pink cheeks.

As she slept, Mr Cameron glanced at her from time to time. He admired her spirit and her determination, and not for the first time, was aware of his own single state. A wife like Mistress Watson, he thought, would be a very fine thing. He eased his injured arm slightly. Though supported by a sling it still ached mightily. He felt useless, with only one arm functioning. He would have preferred to be on horseback, but this commission did demand a stagecoach ride – check the countryside, check the people in the coach, those joining, those leaving, the wayside inns, even the coachman and his rider. Communications with the enemy took all forms – from quick words, sly glances, papers changing hands – he had to be on the alert all the time.

Ewan Cameron had spent most of the last few years speculating on his companions' activities and characters. He called himself a public servant. In reality, he was an agent for his country, sniffing out traitors, weaklings, information useful to the British side. He liked to think his instincts had been well honed by now, and that he could trust them. And from what his friend Bob Stott had suggested, his growing awareness of that man Setton's actions, his instincts suggested there was a story here.

The coach jogged on, the noise on the box outside calmed down as the vehicle moved along the ragged highway. Inside, the passengers dozed, or thought their own thoughts, twitching and shifting with the movement of the horses. Mary stared through the dusty window. England, it seemed, was much the same as Scotland! The houses were grey or whitewashed, the grass was as green – it might even be the same country, she thought, dozing off again to the steady rhythm of the coach.

She woke with a start. The coach was slowing down. She peered out through the window. It was dark. She eased her cramped limbs.

'Where are we?' she asked of Mistress Scott.

'The waybill said we would stop at Newcastle, Mistress. This is it, where we will sleep the night.'

The door opened, and the coachman let down the steps. Mary struggled to move and stumbled out of the coach.

'Here we are in England, Mistress.'

'It seems strange to me, sir, that our two countries should have been at war in the past.'

'Ah, you know some history, then?' said Mr Cameron.

'Now we are one country, and surely we are the better for it?'

'There are some who would disagree with you,' he said quietly. 'Some who prefer an independent Scotland … and some who would see us bend the knee to France. You have heard, I am sure, of the Auld Alliance – the agreement between the Scots and the French?'

She caught her breath.

'Sir?'

'A long-standing and now perhaps more informal agreement between these two great countries, formed for an effort at controlling the English. I speak no treason, ma'am, but we are at war with France ... and there are some who would belike move us nearer to the French than to England.'

'As to that, sir, I cannot say. I am but a woman, with a woman's understanding.' Although it angered her to pretend to an inferior ability, she deemed it necessary to avoid further discussion. She inclined her head, and moved off. A quick backward glance showed that he stood still, with his gaze fixed on her, his hand tugging at his snowy cravat. His eyes were hooded and brooding, and she felt a sudden surge of fear, a woman alone and unprotected.

Mary walked quickly along the path pointed out by the coach driver.

'There's the inn door, mistress, you'll get some refreshment before bedtime.'

Mistress Scott was in the hallway of the inn. A smoky, cramped room it was too, thought Mary, its panelling dark and stained, its ceiling black with soot. She coughed her lungs clear of smoke.

'It seems, Mistress, that we must share a

room.'

Mary smiled wearily.

'Indeed, Mistress Scott, I am so fatigued that I could lie down on the benches here and sleep.'

Her companion nodded, pulling off her gloves and unbuttoning her jacket.

'A meal first, I'd suggest. Pray come with me into the dining room,' came the quiet voice of Mr Cameron. He checked the long table for space and bowed them to chairs near the fireplace.

'Pray sit with us, sir,' Mistress Scott invited him. He shook his head. 'Nay, ladies, thank you for your kindness, but no doubt you will have much women's talk to share.'

He moved away, his left arm still in its sling, to a seat closer to the centre of the busy room.

A meal, indeed, thought Mary, that was most welcome. She supped her hot soup, chewed the bread that came with it, and began to feel revived.

'Now let us turn in,' said Mistress Scott, when they had eaten well. They mounted the staircase together to a tiny upper room. 'I shall now just find the privy, then I shall get to bed.'

The privy was in a small closet in the hallway.

'I have been in inns where there was only a chamber pot in the rooms, Mistress,' confided Mistress Scott. 'To have a privy is a luxury.'

Mary's nose wrinkled. The privy's smell wafted outside its doors. Inside it was much stronger and she held her handkerchief to her nose.

She dawdled back along the corridor with its worn wooden floor and its wall rubbed shiny by people lurching against it while passing. The bedroom was just as threadbare, with its one big bed covered with a huge blanket. She sat on a chair beside the bed and began to unlace her boots, wriggling her toes free and rubbing her feet.

Mistress Scott groaned.

'Well, at least we've got hot bricks in our bed.' She pulled out a thick woollen nightgown. 'Excuse me, Mistress, I'm going to turn in now.'

Mary laughed.

'It's one person move at a time, Mistress Scott. You go first.'

Her companion failed to see the humour as she squeezed towards her side of the big bed. She sat down and swung her feet on to the bed and looked at Mary, expectantly.

'Am I supposed to help her?' Mary wondered. She looked across at the older woman, leaning back now, with her eyes closed.

'Can I help you, Mistress? You must be very tired.'

'The bumping of the coach has certainly tired me,' admitted Mistress Scott. 'But no, lass, I can manage.' She sat up and began unlacing one boot. Mary moved over to begin unlacing the other. The paper crushed between her breasts crumpled noisily as she leaned down. A quick glance at Mistress Scott reassured Mary that the noise had not been heard. She pulled off the boot and Mistress Scott gave a great sigh of relief. She unlaced her dress, then slid the nightgown over her head.

'Let me help you now.' Mistress Scott leaned over in her turn, and Mary's boots slid off easily. But, fearful of the papers being seen or slipping out of her clothing, Mary refused help with her undressing, with a polite,

'Thank you, ma'am, but I can manage fine.' And she added, 'Like yourself, I am sure, I am eager to get into the warm bed, and to lie straight, and steady, free from the coach's jolting.'

Snuggled down, papers safely tucked under the pillow, she thought, almost unbelieving, this is England. Last night, she'd been in Scotland. As she settled to sleep, she wondered how Maggie was managing, how old Grannie Watson was feeling.

The room was stuffy, but Mary had to hide her face in the blankets to muffle her giggles as her companion began to snore, at first gently, then deeper and deeper. How she and Harry would chuckle over that, she thought, when they were together again. A picture slid into her mind. Harry laughing, lying in bed, his nightshirt rumpled, his hair standing on end. Herself, snuggling into his shoulder, the safe feel of his arms round her. The comforting image of Harry stayed with her until she slept.

'Wash water, mistresses. Wash water!'

It was 6 a.m. when the knock came at the door and both Mary and Mistress Scott sat up startled, hair awry. Mary swung her feet to the floor and stretched out to open the door. She passed the first can of hot water to Mistress Scott, and kept the second one for herself.

'Good morning!' Mary smiled at her companion. 'One night nearer London!'

CHAPTER TEN

Coming down the stairs, she met with Mr Cameron, his sling holding his arm comfortably, just going into the dining room reserved for the stagecoach passengers. He bowed, and held the door open for her. She took her place beside him at the table, and waited while the waiter poured them tea and slammed bowls of porridge down in front of each of them.

'I trust I did not worry you with my comments yesterday?' He shook out his napkin.

'Indeed no, sir, but I would not weary you trying to converse on a subject in which I am wholly ignorant.' She caught his gaze, noted one eyebrow lifted. Did he not believe her, then? 'My own preference in conversation, sir, is limited to recipes, a little reading, and much knitting.'

He smiled.

'Indeed, Mistress Watson, I think you capable of more subjects than that.'

She finished her breakfast.

'Alas, sir, you would be sadly disappointed, I fear. Now I must take a turn about the inn courtyard, to get some fresh air before the next stage.'

He held her chair for her as she moved to the door.

She climbed the stairs to fetch her pack and her cloak.

The courtyard was dirty, the horses snorting as they were put to the traces. The driver saw her, and took her pack, pushing it on to a baggage rack on the roof of the coach.

'We leave in half an hour, mistress, if you want to walk a little first.'

She nodded, and moved out along the road. It was early, with a fine dew still on the roadside. Neighbouring houses had their chimneys beginning to smoke, fires on, cooking breakfast. A small gate led on to a path beside a stream running behind the houses. Mary passed through, lifting her skirts free from the thick mud on the ground. She relished the solitude, the chance to think and have quietness. Though she lived with others, and had a number of friends, still she was someone who craved time on her own. In the coach, she had perforce to be with others, in the inn she had had to share a room and a bed. This solitude in the soft autumn air, with wood smoke scenting the air and dogs barking in the distance – this was what she needed. And even though she relished being alone, she could not help wishing Harry was here to enjoy it with her. Maybe, when she'd found him, they could travel home this way.

It was time to get back to the coach. Sighing, she turned back along the path, slipped through the gate, and walked briskly back to the courtyard. The horses were buckled up, the steps were let down and she climbed into her seat. Mistress Scott was already ensconced, and Mr Cameron climbed in after her.

The conversation in the morning carried on from yesterday's musings. Mistress Scott seemed incapable of thinking of anything else. Would Minnie have had her baby yet, what kind of a time would she have, what kind of labour her mother had had.

'In fact, she might have had it by now,' she confided to Mary, 'because it's been a wee while since I had the last note.' Mary welcomed the talk, for it kept her mind from her own thoughts, and kept her companion focussed on her own life. She was anxious to avoid questions about her own journey, and equally reluctant to manufacture a story. She wondered what on earth she could tell her companion. Luckily, Mistress Scott took it for granted that she was travelling to London to find the same type of 'situation' as 'my wee Minnie did', and Mary was regaled with stories of 'wee Minnie' and her rise from housemaid in the Drysdale household to a cook. 'And she married the head footman, and the Mistress said my wee Minnie could bide on as cook, because she was that good.'

'Oh, that's wonderful.' Mary was sincere in her enthusiasm. It was good to listen to a success story, and hear of someone's happiness. Mistress Scott continued.

'And I'm sure you'll have the same good luck, you have a nice face and a nice way with you.'

The waybill said the coach would change horses at the Derby turnpike, where they would stop for refreshments, then at the Cambridge turnpike, where they would have a small repast. In two more days, they would be in London! She would have to find a room. Mr Stott in Leith had told her to get off the coach at the Limehouse Inn, the first stopping place in London, and the nearest to the docks. She heard his voice in her ears.

'You'll find it a funny place, London, and

folk talk oddly, but that's no' a bad inn. You'll be fine there – mention my name, and say that Chrissie and I were askin' for them.' There must be a whole friendship of innkeepers, she thought, keeping in touch, exchanging information.

Mary stared out the window at the passing English countryside. The rumbling of the coach, the jangling of the reins and the steady clop clop clop of the horses' hooves made a rhythmic background to her unsteady thoughts. She drifted from Harry, ever present in her mind, to Ewan Cameron's comments on France, to the papers she still carried in her bodice. The horses kept up a steady rhythm, and there were no checks on the road. England looked – she had to admit it – much the same as Scotland. The houses were pretty, the streets were clean enough, people dressed much the same way. She drowsed.

But there was a sudden awakening!

Yells and screams from the passengers on top of the coach, hooves thundering round the coach, the windows darkened by a flying black cloak, the coach skidding to a stop, the horses neighing, and the coachman shouting. What was going on? A series of bangs sounded. Were they shots? No – a fist hammering against the side of the coach. Mistress Scott clutched her arm.

'Highwaymen! For sure.' Her voice trembled.

'STAND AND DELIVER.'

Mary shuddered at the raucous command. She made no move, except to shuffle closer to Mrs Scott. Her thoughts were in a whirl. She clutched Mrs Scott's hand. The woman was moaning and wailing.

'What will become of us? Oh, dearie me.' Her sobs might have been audible outside the coach.

Mr Cameron took no notice of his fellow-passengers. His eyes were fixed on the scene outside the coach. His right hand was under his coat at his waist, grasping something Mary guessed at as a pistol. His left hand twitched in the sling as though struggling to be released.

The door handle shook suddenly. Someone must have grabbed it from outside. It wrenched round, but the door remained shut. Mary stared at it in disbelief. They would be stuck inside if the door couldn't be opened. She looked again. There was something pushed through the handle on the inside. Was it a knot? Was the handle tied somehow? She looked round. Mr Cameron glanced at her. She pointed to the handle and he nodded. So he was aware of this extra security, was he? In fact, he must even be responsible for it.

The handle rattled again. Again the door shuddered against the rough attack. Then the highwayman, masked and with a hat pulled low over his brow, bent his face down and looked in.

Mary flung herself back into the corner with a terrified squawk. How could this be? It was Lieutenant Setton!

She was sure. Even the mask covering the face did not disguise those fierce grey eyes. And there was a gun in his hand, pointing at the door.

He couldn't fire, could he? He would hit someone inside, maybe injure more than one of them. Maybe that's what he wanted to do.

But Mr Cameron moved before Setton could. He poked his pistol through the window, and fired.

He must have hit Setton's horse in its hindquarters. There was a scream of anguish as it bucked and tried to rear on its damaged hind legs. But it staggered, and fell. Setton vanished from the doorway, as Cameron struggled to reload his pistol. Mary and Mistress Scott clung even closer, terrified by the noise and sickened by the smell of gunfire.

Mary pointed.

'Look!'

Setton, standing a few yards from the coach, had yanked his own pistol free from his belt and was taking aim. Mr Cameron dropped to the floor.

'Get down, Mistresses, get down between

the seats.'

They loosed their hold on each other. As Mary dropped to the floor, so did Mistress Scott. Hidden from the gunman, Mary thought, but still vulnerable if he chose to fire his pistol into the coach.

Setton shouted, his voice furious.

'Stand and deliver! I want the passengers out! Out, I say!'

'They are after something important,' Mr Cameron said quietly. 'Why would Lieutenant Setton leave his press gang and don highwayman's disguise? What is he up to?'

She was right, she thought, it *was* Setton. And … could it be herself he wanted? He had searched her room, but had not found the pieces of paper. He must have followed her from Leith to Edinburgh and now … here.

'Will we get out?' Mistress Scott fumbled for her purse and pulled it out. 'Here, sir, take it. It may be sufficient.'

He shook his head.

'Wait, mistress.'

Mistress Scott shuffled to Mary's side. The two women put their arms round each other, leaning back as far as they could against what seemed the safer side of the coach. Cameron stood at the door, effectively masking them.

Setton's shadow darkened the door again. Mary could only think of the papers. They must be valuable. Very valuable indeed, if these were the lengths the man would go to recover them.

More yells sounded from outside the coach. Was there a second highwayman? But no one seemed to be handing over their valuables – had the men in the seats on the roof even got down? Were the shouts merely to frighten? The coach horses were whinnying and prancing, rocking the coach from side to side. The injured horse was lying still. Mary could just see it by peering through the curtained window.

Then a shot rang out.

Mary leaned forward and peered through the chinks in the window curtain, flapping in the movement. Yes, she could see there was a second highwayman. He was leaning over his saddle, his gun dropping from his fingers and blood oozing from his fingers. Who had done the shooting? It couldn't have been Mr Cameron, still there beside them. She could only see the two highwaymen, the wounded one and Setton. He was still pointing his gun at their window, but he was looking instead at his injured companion. Another shot sounded, and this time she was sure it came from the coachman. Setton swung his gun round to point again at the coachman. Would he retaliate?

But the injured highwayman shouted something that seemed to make Setton change his mind. He casually discharged his loaded pistol into his injured horse's head. Mary felt sick.

'Tis better that way, Mistress,' Cameron reassured her. 'The horse would die anyway: the wound was too big to heal.'

They watched, hardly daring to breathe, as Setton then climbed up behind his companion highwayman and they backed off, horse whinnying in protest at the double load. Mary was shocked. Were they just to let the men escape? Why did the coachman or Cameron not finish off the highwaymen? She looked the question.

'I dislike killing, ladies,' said Cameron, putting his pistol on the coach floor. 'And it is illegal for the coachman to do so.'

He banged on the coach side.

'Drive on! Drive on, I say. They're moving off.'

Mistress Scott gave a gasp as the coach lurched forward, but Mary was numb. Her hand went to her bodice, but Mr Cameron, turning, shook his head.

'No, Mistress! It may be of inestimable value.'

How could he know what she was carrying? And its possible value? Had he been in Sillery to find out about Lieutenant Setton, who carried some notes in French concealed in the lining of his coat? How much did Mr Cameron know?

The coachman was driving on, fast and furiously, the horses panting and puffing, the hooves thundering. Mr Cameron sank back into his seat. He looked slightly dishevelled.

'We have left them far behind, ladies. Nothing now to worry about.'

He pushed his hair back into its usual neat waves, and wiped his brow with a large white handkerchief. Instinct told her again to trust this man. He had saved her from Lieutenant Setton, but she wanted something more, maybe a sign of some sort, something to say, 'We're on the same side.'

The coach slowed its hectic pace to a steadier one, and eventually they reached their next stopping place to change horses. No one spoke as they got out of the coach. The men from the roof seats climbed down and stood in the inn's courtyard.

She slid out of her seat and down the steps before Mistress Scott could say 'We'll go together'. A bit of fresh air, and quiet, she must have!

A side gate from the inn's stable yard led to a small orchard where a pig snuffled under the trees.

She drew two or three deep breaths, feeling her shoulders ease, her head clear just a little. Then came a voice.

'Why the haste, Mistress Watson?' Ewan Cameron was leaning against the gate. He smiled as he saw her expression. 'Yes, I have appeared again, and you thought you'd escaped everyone.'

Good heavens, the man could read her thoughts.

'You are right, sir, I need some solitude and fresh air after our recent escape.'

'But it may not be safe for Mistress Watson to go by herself.' His voice was soft. 'And the ground is rough. You need an escort.'

She turned abruptly.

'Sir, I do not wish to argue with anyone, especially a travelling companion who has saved my life, but I would prefer that I walked by myself.'

'But safely, too.' Ewan Cameron strolled beside her. She ignored his proffered arm.

'I do not feel unsafe now, sir.'

'Mistress Watson, so much is evident. Yet our highwayman friends may not give up.'

He voiced her own fears.

'We may need to join forces, don't you

think?'

She chose to ignore his words, and stooped to pick a small flower.

'See, how pretty. A small red pimpernel.'

'You are fond of flowers, Mistress?'

'I am indeed.'

The ground was indeed rough, and she was forced to take his arm as they turned back to the coach. Her thoughts were whirling. Every word this man said hinted at some knowledge. But of what? Maybe she was misinterpreting everything, putting them into a context of her limited knowledge.

Perhaps she was misjudging him. Yet he had been in Sillery.

They neared the coach, and she stumbled slightly. He steadied her.

'There are many slips, Mistress, are there not?'

'Thank you, sir, I will watch my step ... very carefully.'

They reached the inn where the new horses were being backed into place, and harnessed to the coach.

'First of all, a dish of tea,' he suggested. Mistress Scott was at the door of the inn and beckoned to them.

'Tea has been bespoke, sir, Mistress Watson.'

The break was welcome, the tea refreshing. And it was peaceful to be in the spacious inn rooms. She began to feel better after the ordeal. It had been terrifying, but the highwaymen had been defeated and she had not given up anything.

Now it was back to the confines of the coach. A further quick turn about the yard and Mary was ready to climb in again.

Mistress Scott was already in place, and drowsing, as Mary sat down. She had a tendency to lean towards Mary who drew as far as possible into her own corner. She was sure she would never doze off, so afraid was she of another encounter with the highwayman. What would have happened had he managed to pull her out of the coach? Her imaginings kept her awake long after her companions drowsed.

Eventually she herself became drowsy, slumping in her corner seat, hanging on to the strap by the window. For a few miles every lurch and jerk of the coach roused her. But, at last, she slept thoroughly.

Another stopping place, another inn, another night on the road, and London was in sight. Three days, or was it four, she asked herself.

'I am losing track of time,' she said to her companions. 'We seem to have been on the road so long.'

Mr Cameron smiled.

'We are nearly there, Mistress Watson. After this night's rest, we arrive in London tomorrow. A good journey, on the whole.'

She shook her head with a smile.

'Nay sir, a highwayman stop does not make for a good journey.'

'But he gained nothing, Mistress,' chimed in Mistress Scott. 'We were fortunate.'

Mary was forced to agree.

CHAPTER ELEVEN

Mary was dreaming, dreaming of Harry and herself, hand in hand through the streets, running down to the stony beach. Then the jolting of the coach took on a new note and she was jerked back to the harsh realities of driving into early morning London.

The coach was rattling through the London streets and the noise over the cobblestones was deafening. The pavements were thronged with a mass of hurrying, scurrying humanity. Small boys dodged nimbly in and out of the crowds, hawkers shouted their wares, women held their skirts in and clung to their reticules, walking purposefully to the shops, while men pushed their way through the crowds, some with thoughtful frowns and others with an air of leisure. The prolonged roar of humanity, and the hustle and bustle of the crowded pavements stunned Mary into horrified silence. She'd never imagined it could be so busy, so full of people. How was she going to manage here? By herself? What had she done? Maybe she could go straight back home again?

The coach seemed to take forever to get through the streets. The cries of street sellers, the noise of horses, the clatter of the hooves and the rumble of the wheels jolted her almost unbearably. She thought,

'We'll never get clear of this.'

She must have spoken aloud, because Mistress Scott was nodding, hands to her ears, and Mr Cameron was smiling almost as if he understood and shared her horror of the bustle.

Nothing softened the harsh streets. No trees, no plants, no pleasing buildings, only this stupefying mass of hurrying people, looking neither to right nor left, a never-ending movement of grey faced, grey clad mannikins.

She gripped her hands together, willing herself not to cower in the corner but to stay upright and at least seeming to be in charge of her situation. In his corner, from half-closed eyes, his face a mask, Ewan Cameron watched her.

The coach eventually stopped.

'It seems we have arrived, Mistresses.' Cameron spoke quietly, his voice breaking the sudden stillness of the coach.

Mary eased her cramped limbs, straightened her bonnet, rearranged her tumbled skirt, and stepped off the coach, on to London ground. The air was fresh and cool after the stuffiness of the coach. It smelled of the sea.

Well, at least she'd reached her destination.

She felt very vulnerable and visibly alone as she got down from the coach. Mistress Scott followed her off the coach and was immediately enveloped in a small group of women, excitedly talking, patting and hugging her. She pulled free and waved to Mary.

'Goodbye! Good luck!'

As the women walked off Mary felt lost indeed, without a friend in the world. She turned to pick up her pack. It wasn't there! She looked down in horror at the unloaded baggage. Where was hers? This was the last straw! She felt like weeping.

A touch on her arm startled her.

'I have your baggage, Mistress, safe and sound.' Mr Cameron smiled down at her as though he knew of her fear.

'What … what …' She was about to say, 'What right have you?' but held back. Why was he always so helpful?

'Let me carry it for you into the Inn,' he suggested, and walked with her up the pathway, a bag in each hand.

Someone, a potboy maybe, was holding the door open.

She walked uncertainly into the dimly lit passage. Mr Cameron followed, set down the bags, and shouted,

'Landlord!'

'Wotcher want?' A voice greeted them harshly. A small balding head bobbed out from a back room.

'If you please, sir,' she began, but Mr Cameron raised his hand.

'We require a room each for a night or two, landlord.'

Mary refused to be left out of this exchange. She added,

'Mr Stott from Edinburgh ...'

'You know Bob Stott?' The colour of the voice changed towards her from coldness to warmth, and there was a gap-toothed smile as well. 'Come in, come in and welcome.'

Mr Cameron grinned at her.

'Good for us, yes, Mistress? We know the

right people.'

She thought she detected a slight Scottish accent in the landlord's speech. It made her feel at home. He gazed up at her.

'Come this way,' he commanded, his voice sounding too large to come from such a small body. He seized her pack and ran off, his bowed legs carrying him fast. Speed was essential, for some reason, Mary thought, as she gathered her skirts and hurried after him. The Inn was much dirtier than Bob and Chrissie Stott's Leith inn. The room was tiny, little more than a big cupboard, with a bed with odd looking, rumpled sheets. The little man dumped her pack and winked at her. 'Stay here ...'

She watched him dart through the doorway and stared as he ran down the passageway. His funny waddling gait – in a small man with a big body, tiny legs, and a big head – made him an odd figure, a figure of fun, but somehow Mary sensed an underlying strength. Maybe, she mused, that's because he knows Bob Stott. If Bob Stott recommends him, surely I can trust him.

She turned to the bed, wrinkling her nose in disgust. The sheets were crumpled, the blankets wrinkled and spotted. When she took a couple of steps to a table which was all the small room would allow, it was so dusty she could write her name on it. She pulled out the tail of her shawl and drew it lightly over the top. Scots poverty hadn't accustomed her to such dirt and decay. She laid down her pack on the cleaned surface, and smoothed her dress over her hips. Underneath the table was a chamber pot, and a ewer of water stood in a basin. She poured a little of the cold liquid into the basin – clean, she was thankful to see – and washed her face and hands. She dried her face lightly on her towel, and brushed her hair.

The doorknob clicked, and she turned sharply. Someone was trying to push the door open. Mary had had the forethought to wedge her cloak against the door, but it wouldn't hold for long. The door pushed again, dislodging the cloak. She leaned her full weight against the wood before calling out,

'Who is it?'

'It's me, Mistress, Bob Stott's friend.'

Good! Mary thought, and pulled the cloak clear.

The little man came in.

'It's maybe none of my business, Mistress, but I'd like to ask a few questions, find out your lay.' His directness felt almost rude. She stared.

'My lay?'

He grinned, a gap-toothed black toothed grin.

'What you're up to, Mistress, what a young woman like you is doing here. And friendly with Bob and Chrissie Stott, too. A young woman travelling by yourself, and so far from your home, if I mistake not. You're not, if you get my drift, our usual sort of customer. And the man who came in with you, Mr Cameron, he said you'd had a bit of a dust-up with a highwayman.'

She looked at him steadily.

'I'm joining my husband. He's in the Navy, and I ... I want to find him ... to say fare thee well.'

Why had she blurted that out? Maybe it was the unwavering gaze that held hers, a gaze which shrewdly seemed to reach behind her eyes to her mind.

'That's only part of it,' he said softly. 'You're trying to find your man – he was pressed, like as not. We have a few women who come to look for their men. But there's more?'

Why was he asking? What was he thinking? What had Mr Cameron told him? She felt sorely unprotected and vulnerable. Maybe she could wedge the door, sleep out the night and get the first coach back home in the morning. Why had she ever come on this adventure?

'What more should there be, landlord?' She was surprised to find her voice steady. He ignored the question.

'What ship's your man on?' he asked.

Her mind was in a whirl. Supposing he was hand in hand with Lieutenant Setton. Supposing Lieutenant Setton was still following her? All she wanted now was to get rid of that paper, to feel safe again, not to be attacked for a scrap of information.

'What ship?' he asked again.

She struggled to find her tongue.

'I don't know,' she stammered. She'd had an exhausting and frightening trip. Mr Cameron had saved her life, she was sure. But why? Did he want something from her too?

'I don't know, I don't know, I don't know!' She came near to shouting. 'I don't know the ship, I don't know when he'll get here ... I don't know if we'll ever find each other again. And I don't know if we'll ever get back home together – safely.'

She could have added, I don't know who I can trust, but he guessed at that and said,

'You can trust me, Mistress. I'm Jem, and Bob Stott and I were mates years ago on an old ship ... it's quite a story but I'll not bother you with it now.'

Again, there was a hint of Scots in his tone. She felt reassured again and a little calmer.

'Aye, Jem, Harry was pressed. How can I find him? What can I do?'

A short summary. But behind the words lay a myriad of emotions. Love, hope, fear, sadness, despondency. She'd set off on what she dreaded was a wild goose chase. Not knowing London, not knowing the dockyards, not knowing anyone to ask – what had she been thinking of? Fear showed in her face.

Jem was quick to reassure her again.

'I have ways and means, Mistress, I'll ask about ... and while I'm about it, I'll tell you where you can go and who you can meet. You have to be careful round here.'

She nodded, gratefully.

'Get you down to the small parlour by the dining room, and I'll give you something to eat, then you can have a sleep the long night, and I'll see what I can find out for you.'

'But before then ...' Another voice spoke from the doorway. It was Mr Cameron! 'There are men to look out for. We may have a name, Jem – there's a Lieutenant Setton who seems to be important, and Mistress Watson here,' he smiled at her, 'seems to have some attraction for him.'

Jem nodded.

'That's someone we'll be looking for, aye. Lieutenant Setton.' He repeated the name, as if getting to know it.

Mr Cameron waved a hand as if inviting her to leave her room.

'First of all, we need to meet – the three of us. In your office, landlord, if you please, and immediately. There is no time to lose – either for us or for Mistress Watson here.'

Jem's eyes narrowed.

'Ah yes, sir, that's a fact.' He turned to go. 'Come with me, Mistress.'

A woman with two men? In a private office? She misliked this, but Mr Cameron seemed very determined – and if this business with Setton was connected with Harry, then maybe it could help her, too. And Mr Cameron was right: she was in a hurry. But still she hesitated. Mr Cameron turned back.

'We need to gather and exchange our news, Mistress, and methinks you are an important part of this.'

Knowing what lay hidden in her bodice, she could not deny it. What had she got herself into? Heart pounding, and still dazed from the travel, she followed him, waiting as he locked her door. How would she ever find her way round this maze of intrigue? She felt almost overwhelmed by events. She stiffened her spine, gritted her teeth.

'I never thought it would be like this. I thought I'd just get into the docks, and ask ... I never thought of all this.' And she made a sweeping gesture round the inn and its shabby surroundings.

Jem looked as if he might pat her shoulder but thought it might be somewhat over-familiar. He contented himself with grunting,

'It's new to you, it's new, and new things take a bit of learning. But, Mistress, you can trust us, Mr Cameron and myself. We will help in times of need.' He set off down the corridor at his odd gait. 'Come downstairs and get some food in you as we speak.'

CHAPTER TWELVE

Cautiously, Mary followed Jem along the passage to the stairway. She descended, hand holding the banister rail lest she slip on the uneven surfaces. She suspected the wooden steps were cracked, and the bare plaster walls felt damp. She'd never been in such a dirty beggarly place. But there was no going back.

She followed him towards his office at the front of the inn. In the doorway stood Ewan Cameron. He made her a bow.

'We must talk, Mistress Watson, the three of us. Our business concerns you ... and your husband.'

She stood still, her eyes narrowed, her

breath coming faster.

'I do not understand.'

'Come with me, Mistress, into our good friend Jem's office.'

Into a room on her own with two men? Was that how things were done in London? But if Mr Cameron had information about Harry … Oh Harry, Harry, if only I could reach you, she thought. I want to rescue you, or be with you, but – She could not finish the thought. Or perhaps she dared not. Determination was part of her character, but there were times when she knew she had not counted or was not aware of the cost of that determination.

Once more, despite Jem's efforts at reassurance, she felt totally out of her depth, among people of a strange speech, in a city which she did not know. But having come so far, there was no turning back. She forced herself to remember how well she had managed up to now. She'd got herself from Sillery down to London, hadn't she? Kept the papers secret? And survived an encounter with highwaymen! She lifted her chin, and followed Mr Cameron, perforce, into Jem's dingy little office.

He set aside two chairs for them just out of sight of the window which gave on to the passageway. Jem's seat was just underneath the window.

'We need to talk, to share information, and maybe, to plan, since we will have a battle on our hands,' Mr Cameron said. He looked quizzically at Mary. 'Mistress, I can see your fear. Of me, of the situation, of all that might happen. Natural enough! But you need not be afraid of myself nor of Jem. We are on the same side, I believe. And we need to trust each other.' Privately, he felt he could trust her. As well as leaving her home and looking out for her husband, she seemed to be fighting off Setton, a man who aroused all his suspicions. Surely this all added up to someone he could trust. And admire, he thought, trying to brush aside thoughts of her glossy dark hair, clear dark eyes and – even – her contrary nature, going against all he had been taught that a woman should be. And he badly wanted to know what she had that Setton seemed to want. He remembered the paper he'd managed to rip, and he knew that a woman had been picking up the other part. He was sure it was Mistress Watson who had grabbed the other papers. And at least one was part of an incriminating document.

She looked back at him, weighing him up again, hesitating, heart thumping.

'How can I tell that, sir?' Mary pushed aside a drooping lock of hair. She felt she'd been living in a little bubble she called 'Fife' – where she knew everyone, their thoughts and predictable actions.

She'd carried those feelings with her, believing that Fife was a microcosm of the world, and that her knowledge of Sillery and the villages around was a sufficient preparation for travel.

Now she knew how wrong she was, how naive she had been, how stupid. And how right had been the folks back home when they said, 'don't go.'

Ewan Cameron was watching her. She felt he could read her mind. He proved it by saying,

'It's not quite like home, is it?'

She could only shake her head.

Jem intervened.

'Sit you down here, Mistress. Mr Cameron will help. I will guarantee it.'

She sat, she could do nothing else, and waited, hands clenched in her lap.

Ewan Cameron pulled out a document from one of the capacious pockets in his greatcoat. He looked straight at her.

'Mistress Watson, I know something of your story.'

She froze.

'You are here to find your husband who was pressed, of course. I guessed you came from Sillery, for some information on, ah, interesting activities had come my way, and I had gone to Fife to investigate. There, I found a press gang in action, led by a certain naval lieutenant – one whom you and I have met again, Mistress. One who seems to have an interest in you.'

She nodded.

'You must know something or have something he wants? You indicated as much to me on the coach when Setton played his highwayman role.'

She thought fleetingly of the papers tucked into her bodice and nodded again.

Cameron shrugged off his greatcoat, leaned forward and spread some pieces of paper on the small table.

'Mistress, this is something you will forget you have seen ... we are not in Sillery now, but in the middle of something so big that we are like tadpoles swimming in the ocean amongst the great big sharks. But remember, our instincts, our knowledge of people, and, dare I say it, our integrity that comes from a good country, a good home and good people ... that will be the basis for our success.'

Jem rubbed his hands.

'That's quite a speech, Mr Cameron.'

Ewan Cameron turned, his broad shoulders

straight under his coat of fine blue cloth.

'And I mean it, Jem. Without our home-taught love of justice and peace, and care for each other, neither you, nor I, nor Mistress Mary here would be together. Nor would we be trying to help each other and confound the traitors to our fair land.'

Mary felt better. Maybe he had intended that. But she felt she had regained her steadfast purpose: finding Harry, who had been so unjustly taken. And confusion to Lieutenant Setton, she thought.

She leaned forward as he spread a further fragment on the small table between them. It looked like the paper she had but part of a larger piece, with torn edges. Could there be any fit with the piece she still held in her bodice? She wanted to try to match them up. Could she risk it?

She struggled to read the words underlined by Cameron's pointing finger. He read them out loud in French for her and for Jem.

'Setton .... partisan ... le paiement sera ... 1,000 francs.' He translated: 'Setton. A partisan ... payment will be ... 1,000 francs.' Cameron moved his finger down the paper, his eyes hooded in concentration. 'There is no signature, it is missing – two pieces, maybe more, torn off, it seems – perhaps in Sillery?' He met her eye with a slight smile. 'Nor is there any detail of the services rendered. But there are some names here, and we suspect the passing on of naval intelligence. You see, Mistress, we are caught up in great things …' His brown-eyed glance was direct. 'And I am trusting you.'

Her mouth was dry. Her heartbeats thundered in her ears. She wondered if she dared speak. If she did, what might be the consequences? She looked up at last.

'Sir, I am not to be tangled so. I am here only to find my husband, and if possible, to aid him to freedom. I do not wish to be caught up in such matters.'

Ewan Cameron bowed his head.

'I respect that, Mistress, but may I ask again, why is our friend following you? Would it not be better, if you wish to focus on finding your husband, to rid yourself of any other encumbrances you might have?'

Jem was a friend of Mr Stott's, Mr Cameron seemed to be a friend of both. The paper fragments Mr Cameron showed her and his words about passing secrets to the enemy implied that their loyalties tallied. She made up her mind.

'I want no more of this, sirs. Excuse me!' Turning her back on the men, she reached down into her bodice and pulled out the papers. She turned back to them. 'This, sirs, I believe to be the reason. And I want rid of it.'

Mr Cameron nodded. He had remembered correctly. She was the one who had spilled the paper on to the ground during a scuffle with the press gang leader. He reached out for the half sheet of paper and smoothed it on the table. Jem leaned forward eagerly. Mary continued.

'He was on his horse in Sillery to lead the press gang that took my Harry. I was caught up by his horse, and had to fight my way free. I caught his coat and ripped the lining with its pocket as he dragged me forward. I must have ripped the paper as well, and this piece fell out.'

Jem looked at her wonderingly.

'You … grappled with a naval officer?'

She nodded.

'He was pushing me with his horse, sir, and I feared to fall under the hooves. So I grasped the tails of his coat for safety.' She added, 'He was wearing a long-tailed coat, otherwise …' she hesitated, 'I might not be here now. I might have been crushed under the horse's hooves.'

Jem cackled loudly, showing rotten stumpy teeth in his open mouth. He put his hand to his lips.

'Apologies, Mistress, but the thought of you

tackling a naval lieutenant, and on his horse too, makes me want to laugh. It's daft, that's what it is, just plain daft!'

Cameron raised his hand.

'But incredibly courageous. I salute you, Mistress.'

'Thank you. I feared for my life, believe me. We were all involved back there in Fife.'

He nodded.

'I saw that.'

Mr Cameron bent over the paper, watched by Jem and by Mary. He slid it into position, matching it up with the torn edges of the other segments. It fitted perfectly. There was almost a whole sheet. Jem grinned and glanced at Mr Cameron.

'That's it, then?'

'We surely have a major piece of the puzzle,' Mr Cameron said, tracing the words with his forefinger. 'Look at this!'

Mary and Jem peered over the paper with him.

'Bonaparte,' read Jem slowly.

'This is enough to damn Setton with his superiors and to get him and his comrades out of harm's way. May I keep this paper, please, Mistress?' Cameron laid his hand firmly over it.

She nodded.

'An it please you, sir, I am happy not to have hold of it. But, please tell me, what does it all say?' She touched her bodice briefly, making sure she looked respectable. It still held the Exemption Certificate which was to free Harry, she hoped.

He hesitated.

'With your piece added, I believe I have now got the full paper, and I can manage the full translation. It looks as if a general on behalf of Bonaparte authorises the bearer of this note a sum of 1000 francs in payment of services rendered.'

'How is it connected to our friend, sir?' Jem entered the conversation again.

'It names Setton as a partisan, just here.' He pointed. 'And there are other names which must be connected, too.' Mr Cameron lifted his hand and pointed to the list of names. The two men looked at each other. 'This certainly links a number of people with the Friends of the French,' Mr Cameron mused. 'I wonder what services might be demanded.'

'Careless, sir,' commented Jem. 'Why would he be carrying it around with him? Why would it be tucked into his coat pocket?'

'That is what we have to find out. Could it be that …'

Mary had had enough. She was not interested in spy-catching. She had but one purpose in mind. She stood up, smoothed her skirts, and turned to Jem.

'Sirs, I leave that to you. It is not my purpose. Landlord, Jem, if you please, I would wish some speech with you, regarding how best to walk in these parts and to find the Navy ships.' She looked at him steadily. 'You said you knew.'

Jem looked at Mr Cameron, received a nod, and got up.

'Come to the door, Mistress, and I will show you.'

Mr Cameron began to fold the paper again. She turned to him.

'I bid you good day, sir.'

CHAPTER THIRTEEN

She walked to the outside door. Jem followed.

'You will not go out by yourself, Mistress,' he said firmly. 'Let me find someone to go with you.'

'Point me the way to find my husband, please, Jem, and I will step as briskly as I can.'

'It is not seemly ... nor,' he said, 'is it safe. Please to remember, Mistress, that Admiral Lord Nelson is organising the fleet to go into battle. And that dockyards are not the most respectable of places.'

'I will be careful, Jem, I promise you. But I have a purpose and will step firmly. Please point the quickest way to where the ships might be.' She sounded, at least, energetic and determined. But she felt almost stupefied by the number of people, the strangeness of the language, the buildings, and, she acknowledged to herself, the dirt. As for the battle, she pushed that to the back of her mind. Immediate and in the forefront was to find Harry.

His gaze sharpened and he stared at her, probing her feelings, checking her words. She longed to be back home among familiar surroundings and friends. But Harry came first. And, in truth, she felt an excitement, a zest for his nearness, imagining his expression as he saw her, wondering how she could get close to him. Fearful, yes indeed. But also wasn't there a strong frisson of adventure?

She moved outside with Jem. The air smelt of dockyards, and sea, and some unmentionable smells, dirt, decay, old buildings, filthy streets. Her eyes narrowed and she stared around. Jem pointed to the right.

'The docks, Mistress, are straight down from here, and you will find the ships easily.' A shout from inside made him turn back into the inn. 'Mind, Mistress, do not stray! Wait for me.'

But Mary had no intention now of staying put in the inn.

'I am no bairn to be nursed,' she said firmly. 'I will walk down this street and up again, and I will not stray off the path.'

Jem's grimy hand went to his mouth.

'No,' he whispered roughly. 'No, you

should not ...' He turned back to the inn. 'I will tell someone to go with you.'

'No!' She was resolute. She felt that there was no more time to waste. But Jem still hesitated. The shouts grew louder.

'I have to go and attend to business. Mistress, please, be careful. Do not venture far. Keep to this main street. These can be dangerous parts.'

But she had come this far. She had managed coach travel, strange inns, and highwaymen. Now she was near her goal. She was resolved. Find Harry! And Jock, and Archie Stott – for a moment she almost giggled. How many pressed men could she rescue?

This was not, she knew, the broad highway the coach had arrived by. The road to the docks was rougher, badly surfaced and worn. She stepped slowly away from the inn door, for it was already a difficult walk. She moved carefully, lifting her skirts to avoid she knew not what, and only glanced up now and again to make sure of her route. The houses were grimy, the doorways broken, kicked, knife-scarred. There were few in the doorways, few in the street. But she felt eyes on her back. People were watching her, she was sure. A shiver of alarm crept up her spine, and she straightened her shoulders against it. Maybe she should turn back. But no! She had come to find Harry. She would ask the first person she saw where the Navy ships were docked.

A slatternly woman slouched in one doorway, clay pipe dangling from her lips, coarse, greasy hair, dirty apron, and sloppy down at heel shoes. She stared impudently at Mary from half closed eyes. Mary drew a deep breath.

'If you please, mistress ...'

She got no further.

'Eeeh!' the woman screeched. ''Ark at 'er! Don't she talk funny?'

Huh, Mary thought, it's you who talks funny.

She tried smiling.

'I'm looking for the Navy ships, to find my husband, he was ... taken ... I'm from Scotland, come down on the coach.'

'Pressed, wuz 'e? You'll never fin' im.'

'But I would like to try. Please can you tell me the way to where the Navy ships are docked?'

'Nah ... no place for the likes o' you.' The woman spat on the ground and moved back inside the house.

Mary groaned. Better luck next time. Or should she turn back?

The street veered to the right, and she followed. The smell of the docks was stronger. Maybe she was within a street or two? She stood, staring round her. Was this definitely the way? How could she go straight if the street didn't?

BANG! She was jolted along, with a push between her shoulder blades that sent her staggering.

'What ... what ... who?'

She turned. There was no one to be seen. But as she stared round the street, she thought she glimpsed a tousled dark head, small, maybe a child.

Odd, she thought, but then children do odd things.

She turned back to go along the street again. And again, she felt a push.

This time she spun round quickly. She'd almost been expecting it, almost waiting for it. This time, she had her hand out and grabbed. And she caught the wrist of a dark tousle-headed child.

'What's this about?' she demanded. 'How dare you push ... and me a stranger here?'

'That's why, we don' wan' no strangers 'ere.'

'But there must be lots of strangers around the docks!'

'Then we don' wan' you here!'

'I mean you no harm.'

The child twisted his arm free.

''Ow do we know that?' he demanded over his shoulder, as he ran off.

Mary made a face. Maybe Jem was right, maybe she should turn back.

But when she turned, she found herself struggling to recognise the houses.

'If I go straight back this way …' she thought.

But it wasn't so easy. In her haste, and her concentration on the smell of the dockyards getting stronger, she hadn't noticed streets jutting off the main roadway. Some streets were full of stalls and stallholders, others empty of anyone.

She stood at a kind of crossroads, bewildered.

'Got yoursel' lost, 'ave you?'

'Yes.' Mary turned and met the eyes of a young woman, her own height, but dressed in such a style as made Mary blush.

'Well, we don' care. You be off where you came from, you're only 'ere for one thing.'

'I'm here to find my husband,' Mary began.

'Gwan, tell us another one.'

This came from a different woman who had joined the first. More women came out from behind the narrow battle-scarred doorways. Mary groaned in fear.

'I *am* here to find my husband. He was pressed. I've come down after him from Scotland.'

'A likely story.'

'Oh yeah, believe that one, would you?'

'Come on, you can do better than that.'

'We've just enough custom to go round – we don't need more competition 'ere.'

The women pressed forward and Mary tried to stand her ground, but she was forced to give way. Stepping backwards, she raised her hands, palms outwards. What were they going to do to her?

'Please, believe me ...' she whispered.

The leaders got nearer, and the stench from their unwashed bodies and garments reeked in her nose until she thought she'd be sick. Her back pressed against a wooden surface. She was surrounded now, the leaders reaching for her shawl, her bonnet, the charm that Harry had given her.

'That's mine, Harry gave it me.'

'Ow, get 'er, 'Arry give it 'er.'

The hands were holding her, pulling her about, pulling her hair, slapping her face.

'NO, NO, NO!' Mary yelled. She pulled free, turned and slipped between the leaders and raced off down the nearest street, clutching her bonnet.

'Let 'er go, go on, let 'er go!' came from behind her.

'No! We don' wan' anyone else round 'ere!' And Mary felt clods of mud and something else hit her across her back and shoulders. A boy – maybe the same boy? – swung down from a windowsill and spat on her shoulder. She put a hand up groggily, to wipe away the spit.

Were they following? They seemed to be close. What could she do to escape?

Even as she wondered, a hand came out of a doorway and grabbed her. It swung her round and inside a building. Someone had come to her rescue! The door slammed against the women, and she fell against it, gasping for breath.

The hall was empty, and dim. Only the figure of her rescuer stood there close to her, towering over her. Could it be Mr Cameron? Could it be – she swallowed – Harry?

'Now, mistress – my paper.'

Setton!

'No,' she whispered. 'No, no, not you. No. Let me go.'

'What? Let you go back into that mob? You're safer with me. Give me my paper!'

His voice was hoarsely menacing. He loomed over her, his lips tight as he spat out the words. Outside she could hear the voices of the women, fading as they gave up on their chase. She made as if to open the door and he grabbed her again, and spun her round with her back against him, her arms twisted behind her.

'Where's that bit of paper?'

'Na! Not here. I haven't got it.'

'You have! And I need it!' He gave an extra squeeze to her arms.

Her English words deserted her. She screamed loudly in Scots.

'Na! Na! Na! Dinna! Dinna!'

His right hand gripped her throat and the screams died to a gurgle. She wrenched an arm free, with the sound of cloth ripping. His hand moved across her throat to her shoulder and he twisted her arm back behind her. Tears spilled down her cheeks.

The pain was excruciating.

'The paper!' he yelled in her ear.

She screamed again, this time from the pain.

The noise of battering hands at the door made her pause. The door was beginning to swing from its hinges. The yells grew louder. The women were back.

'We'll get her!'

God help her! She was between the villain and the women!

She screeched, terrified. She yelled in Scots, louder, her voice sounding shrill and fierce.

'Na, na, na! Dinna! Dinna!! He's got me! An' I canna get oot!'

'HOLD ON!' There was a shout from amongst the crowd. The crowd went silent. And another young woman yelled through the doorway.

'Where do ye come frae?'

'FIFE! Sillery!' Mary yelled back, trying to twist her mouth from Setton's cruel grip. What did it matter now where she came from? She might never see home again! Setton's left hand explored her gown, looking for pockets, and she tried to drag her skirts away.

The voices outside were hard to hear as she

concentrated on struggling to free herself. Setton, unable to discover the paper, was furious. She pulled and wriggled against his hands. He wrenched her arms behind her, gripping her wrists with one hand. She screamed again, and his other hand grabbed her throat.

'My paper, Mistress. Give!'

'Haven't … got … it,' she gasped against his suffocating grip. She writhed and struggled. Every muscle ached but she kept on wrestling against his grip.

He pulled her back along the filthy passage, dragging her at his heels as she fought and yelled.

'You know where it is. I mean to have it.' Her head snapped back as he shook her furiously.

There was an enormous crash, and a cascade of shouts and yells as the women burst in along the passage, surrounding them, pulling at Setton's arms, kicking at his legs.

He released his grasp and she stumbled against the dank rough wall, putting out a hand to save herself from falling. As she struggled to pull herself upright, Mary felt herself grabbed again, and pulled back towards the open door. The women surrounded her. They must be mad.

The mob dragged her back towards the

street. Some of the women were running after Setton who had disappeared along the filthy passage. Distantly she could hear their shouts and his running feet, and doors slamming. He was gone.

CHAPTER FOURTEEN

She slumped against the wall, gasping, and trying to pull her torn sleeve up to her shoulder. Her arms ached from being dragged along, but there was to be no rest.

'C'mon, you.' The leader's breasts were half-falling out of her ragged shift. Her dress, torn and tattered as it was, still had some style as it swung round her hips. Her feet were bare. She came closer to Mary. Her mouth had only about half a dozen teeth, and the woman's breath reeked of alcohol. Mary resisted, but another woman came alongside and grabbed her other arm.

Jostled, and shoved, pulled this way and that, she opened her mouth to shout again.

'You yell, Mistress, and I'll shut you up!' the ringleader said. 'You'll get no help from anyone round 'ere. The magistrates don't trouble us.'

Somebody was hissing in her ear. The

Scotswoman again.

'Dinna worry, ye'll be a' right, it's to get ye awa frae him.'

She recognised the accent again.

'Awa?' she whispered.

'Aye, awa. Ye'll be a' right.'

The accent was reassuring. She moved with the crowd. Someone shoved her from behind, other hands kept pulling her arms. Somehow, she stumbled out the doorway. Her sleeves were torn, her her bonnet askew, her hair tumbled down. Nobody would recognise her now as being Mistress Mary Watson. She looked like one of the women's gang. She put a hand up to her head and found the combs which kept her hair in place had gone. But the charm at her neck was still there. Harry's gift, they hadn't taken that.

Harry. With a huge effort she flung off the hands that were holding her.

'I want to find my man! He's on a navy ship. I'm bidin' with Jem.'

'Wuz 'e pressed?'

'Aye, that he was. Him and a wheen o' ithers.'

'Whereabouts in Fife do you come frae?'

'Sillery, on the coast.'

'I'm near Embro.' The woman was fair-skinned and red-haired.

'I thought that.'

The others stood watching the two Scots as they moved together. Mary held out her hand and the other woman closed on it. Her grip was strong.

'Are you really havin' a look for your man?'

'Aye, aye, I am.' Mary reverted again to Scots speech.

'Ah weel, we must do a bit o' helpin'.' Redhead was in charge now.

'But who was that gentleman? Did you know him?' someone demanded.

'Another hoity toity taking without paying, I reckon,' said another woman.

She opened her mouth to explain, then thought better of it. It would take too long, and she was exhausted, and desperate to get to the docks.

She found herself moving along with the group, and they walked back down the street where Setton had found her. Her whole body was aching from the struggle, and she was limping from when Setton dragged her through the passageway. And her mind was in a complete tangle! These women were looking after her! But where were the docks? There were twists and turns in the street until Mary was thoroughly lost. She looked round for her new friend, her Scots acquaintance.

'We havena been introduced ...' she stopped and laughed almost hysterically. 'Sorry, that's a really glaikit thing to say right here and now. But my name's Mary. Mary Watson.'

'I'm Betty ... Betty McGregor.'

'Pleeeesed t' meetchew', said half a dozen English voices, giggling now, and sounding shrill against the Scots' soft accents. Mary raised a hand, ragged sleeve dropping back against her bruised arm. 'Pleased to meet you too.'

Well, she thought, I think I am ... if I can get out of this safely. Maybe Mistress McGregor ... Betty ... will help. She seems to be willing enough. But how can I be sure? What's going to happen? Can I get back to Jem? Will I recognise the streets? Thoughts were spilling through her mind. I wish I'd listened properly to Jem, she thought, I wish I had. But there was no point in regret now. She had no choice but to move along with the women.

And then the group turned a corner, and there was a narrow lane leading straight ahead. Framed at the end of it was a glimpse of polished wood, ropes, cloth – ships, towering ships. The docks at last.

Despite her aches and pains, despite the crowd surrounding her, despite the uneven street, she broke into a run. Harry might be nearby. Harry's ship could be there, must be there! The women were jogging and running beside her.

'That's it! That's it! The docks.'

'Get back, you women!' A man in a scarlet uniform, a sword at his side, came bearing down on them. He looked about eighteen, and full of himself. Mary thought of Bob Stott's missing son Archie.

'Awa with you!' Betty was beside her in an instant. 'We're lookin' for someone.'

'You lot are always on the lookout. No one here for you right now! Be off with the lot o' you. We've got work to do.'

The women scattered, and while he watched, some of them ran back up the narrow cinder-strewn lane, calling and shouting names at him. He began to run after them, but they dodged him, name-calling again, running up behind him, poking him in the back, tugging at his clothes, bobbing up and down, shifting from side to side. He tried to grab one of them, and missed, and they laughed heartily.

'I'll have you all clapped in irons!' the man

cried, but his blushing face did not help him. The women closed round him.

Mary and Betty didn't stop to see the outcome: they took their chance of him being kept well occupied. They slipped up the side of the alleyway into the docks themselves. Big ships, bigger than Mary had ever seen. With rolls of white sail, clean fresh paint, and guns running through big holes in the ships' sides.

'They're beautiful, just ... just beautiful,' Mary murmured.

'Dinna stop, we'll have to have a wee look-see. I ken a man nae far frae here.'

Mary could only follow as Betty led her in and out of narrow alleyways, behind a couple of tavern doors, along filthy gutters, until she stopped at the far end of the dockyards.

'Bobby, are you here?' It was a soft clear call. 'Bobby, Bobby? Where are you?'

There was a shuffling noise and a tall fair young man with a huge slash across his cheek lurched up to them.

'Aw, Bobby, my man.' Betty was in his arms, clinging to him, and hugging him. He embraced her.

'Aye Betty, I'm here, lass, not goin' far.'

Betty took his hand, and held it out.

'Bobby, I've got a friend here. Her name's Mary. She's frae Fife.'

Mary smiled up at the man's face. Then with a shock, she saw his sightless eyes, staring out above her head. She touched his offered hand.

'Hello, Bobby, I'm Mary.'

'Hello, Mary. What're you doin' here? You don't sound as if you belong.'

Betty interposed.

'She's looking for someone.'

'Aye, and that is?'

'A man was pressed – two men, and a lad of eighteen, a main lot from Scotland. They came down frae ...'

Mary filled in.

'From Edinburgh, Bobby, but before then, from Fife.'

'You want me to ask around a bit?'

'Oh yes please, please, please.' Mary's voice cracked. She seemed to be nearer Harry, almost there in fact.

'Min', I can't promise anything, but ... Come back in a couple of hours, maybe around about four o'clock.'

'But will the ships still be here?' Mary asked, worried.

'Oh, aye, they can't leave yet,' said Bobby. 'The tide's not right.'

Of course – a fisherman's wife should have remembered that. She must be more tired than she thought.

'Thanks, Bobby.' Betty hugged him again, and he turned to go, his right hand feeling for the fence along the pathway, a stick in his other hand. Betty saw him safely up the path and turned back to Mary.

'Bobby's my intended. If I ever get out o' this game,' she explained to Mary.

'If I can help, I will.' Mary would have promised Betty anything at that moment, but there was a deeper feeling of care for a woman far from home, with a man who was different.

Betty hugged her.

'Thanks, my friend.'

CHAPTER FIFTEEN

Betty left Mary at the inn where she managed to avoid both Jem and Mr Cameron, and succeeded in tidying herself sufficiently to disguise the mauling she had received. A shawl firmly around her shoulders covered the rip at the top of her sleeve, and even cold water felt good on her grubby hands and face.

And at four o'clock precisely, Betty and Mary walked back along the rough street, now lined with costermongers and their carts. Customers were lining up, jostling, shoving, and buying. Baskets were filled with fruit and vegetables. Preparations for the forthcoming voyage and engagement with the enemy seemed to be in full swing.

The docks were buoyant with men, with horses and carts and mountains of stuff carried on them. The air was tingling with noise, vibrant with activity. Men in uniform, blue for the naval officers and red for the marines, strutted up and down.

Children were following, making faces, playing beside the men, calling names, holding out hands for pennies. Beside one ship's boat, a company of marines was being drilled, holding their rifles by their sides and then ready to fire. By another, two gold-braided men were talking seriously, to judge from their expressions. It looked to Mary's bewildered gaze as if every detail was being thought of. Her own needs, wishes and in fact her own life seemed ordinary and unimportant compared with the swing of preparations for departure.

'They don't want women on their ships. The Admiral, Lord Nelson, forbids it. Doesn't mean there aren't any women though.' Betty returned to her English speech. Mary turned in surprise.

'Why would he not want women on the ship for ... for ...' She hesitated.

'Company? Cooks? Nurses?' Betty shook her head. 'He says no to women, but that disnae mean that there are no women on the ships. Mostly women like me, but some wives are there with their men. That's more for the officers, though.' She made a face, then continued. 'You could go in alongside Harry, but you'd need permission, and that might take a while. Or – now here's an idea - you could dress as a man.'

'As a man?' Mary was dubious, though it was not the first time it had been suggested. Betty nodded.

'We could get you the right clothes.'

Mary gulped.

'Maybe, best find out first the ship Harry and Jock are on. And the lad Archie, too, if he's not long gone.'

Betty shaded her eyes.

'Keep a look out, and just pretend to be strollin' along'.

Arm in arm, the two women paced the docks, as if they were out to take in the views. Boys rushed up to them, laughed at them, danced in front of them and shouted teasing words after them.

Betty shooed them aside.

'They're hungry beggars, poor things, but we don't have much ourselves. And they know it.'

They walked silently along, Mary wondered again at the sights of the London docks, so different from her own small village. Different even from the big docks in Leith. She marvelled at Betty who seemed to be taking everything for granted and who knew where to go, who to speak to, how to speak in English, and more importantly, who to avoid.

'Psst! Psst!' The sound came from their right.

Betty turned slightly, pulling Mary with her, and strolled towards a booth selling sweetmeats. Mary tried to pull back.

'I have no pennies to spare, Betty, my friend.'

Betty ignored her, and smiled and bowed to the shop owner.

'Your pleasure, mistresses,' he invited, spreading one grimy hand above the marchpane and sugar shapes on his counter.

Betty looked closely, keeping Mary's hand firmly tucked in her own elbow. Mary bit her lips. She could not, *would not* spend a groat on such folly. She tried to tug her hand free again, but could not without making a stir.

She caught the owner's gaze. The man's eyes were knowing, and he gave her a half-smile.

'Sir, I cannot be tempted ...'

'Let me show you something else, mistress,' and he leaned forward and said softly. 'Come you round to the right.'

Mary stared. But Betty was tugging at her arm, and they moved from the counter, slowly to the right of the booth. The owner met them there, and pulled them further aside. There was Bobby, Betty's man.

'I got the name for you,' Bobby whispered. 'But there's dark doings afoot. Something's up.'

'The name? You got the name?' Mary wasn't interested in the dark doings. 'The name o' Harry's ship?'

'Aye ... it's *The Talbert*. I'll take you to the bumboats that get you on to the ship itself.'

Mary made as if to start right away, but Betty held her back.

'You can't go right now. Let's just find where it's berthed first.'

'And what are the dark doings?' Mary whispered.

'You may well ask!' Bobby muttered. 'Something's up. Sounds bad. Some of the men are not just too keen to fight the French. Can't say more.'

Mary frowned. Lieutenant Setton came to mind, but she kept her mouth shut.

'Tell me where I can find the ship. Please,' she whispered again.

Bobby took her arm and pulled her gently round to the back of the booth.

'Look up to near the end of this dock. Right up, there's where the boats are. The ones that take the men to the fighting ships.'

'How can you tell?' Mary was bewildered. A blind man giving directions? How?

He smiled and turned his sightless gaze in her direction.

'I wasn't always like this, Mistress, and I have a good memory, and, well, there are other ways of seeing. Smell, feel of cobblestones, hearing, wind on the face – and words, of course.'

She touched his arm gently.

'Thank you.'

The sun glared along a path highlighting the boats and dockyards, lighting the bustling men, casting long shadows behind them as they heaved sacks into the boats, worked on ropes, climbed the riggings. The air rang with the sound of metal on metal, metal on wood, metal on stone.

And through it all, the sailors came and went, running, heaving packs, getting themselves on board the different boats.

The noise was incredible and Mary put her hands to her ears, trying to blot out some of the racket. But her eyes never stopped moving from side to side, up and down the docks, scrutinizing each boat as men moved on to it. Harry was always first in her mind, but following that was Jeannie's Jock, and the memory of the Stotts' kindness, and their anguish for their son.

Betty tugged her arm.

'Have you had enough for now?' she shouted above the turmoil. 'We can come back. *The Talbert*'s boat's right at the far end, we canna get through just at the moment, and you still have time.'

Mary turned.

'Can we not manage a bit more walking? I'll go myself ...' And she started to move forward again, her face grim with determination. 'Just a bit more ...'

Betty was forced to give in.

'That you won't. We'll go together.'

Mary had to admit there was safety in numbers, especially with Bobby there. An indrawn breath, almost too hushed to be heard, made her turn her head.

'I didn't hear, Betty?' she asked, but as she turned to Betty she caught a fleeting glimpse of a familiar figure.

Setton.

She stood still, clutched Betty's arm.

'Stop! Stop!' she hissed to her escorts. 'Stop, that's him! That's Setton. He must have left that wee building where he dragged me.'

They all stared, and then, in her excitement Mary started off towards him, dragging her companions with her.

'Don't you see, he must know where to go, he must know where the men are, he could lead us to Harry.'

'But we know that's the boat, way up there,' said Betty, pointing. Mary could not see its name. But Betty said, 'That's it. That's the boat for *The Talbert.*'

At last!

CHAPTER SIXTEEN

Mary was almost running. Betty dragged at her, trying to slow her down.

'Come on, come on,' panted Mary. 'That's it, that's the boat Bobby said he was on.'

It was a big boat, and yes, *The Talbert* was painted clearly on the bow, in big gold letters.

'That's the boat to take you to the fleet. Got the same name.' Betty told her. She succeeded in stopping Mary's rush. 'Slow down. Slow down. For pity's sake, you'll get us all in trouble, running about like that.'

'But Harry's there, I'm sure. Look.'

Mary pointed towards the stern, where a group of men were huddled together.

They were dirty, ragged and hunched, but one of them had bright red-gold hair.

'Harry's there. He's there. Harry!' She started to run again.

'For goodness' sake, lass, hush. Don't draw

attention to yourself or your man. You don't know what trouble he might get into.'

Mary paused, dragged back by Betty's hands.

'But it's Harry, it is, I saw him. I know it.'

'Fine, fine, fine, lass, but just take it easy, please.'

'For all our sakes,' muttered Bobby.

Slowly she faltered to a halt.

'Harry,' she whimpered. 'Harry. Oh, Harry.'

Betty pushed Mary between herself and Bobby and each with a hand on her arms, they slowly strolled, casually, towards *The Talbert* ferry boat and the huddle of men. Someone was barking out orders. A sailor was giving instructions to the motley bunch – but beside him stood Setton! That familiar stance, that thatch of grey hair, the dark lieutenant's coat. Was he here to hand over his pressed men? Or was there something in this ship connected with the paper she had grabbed? Fitting that paper in with Mr Cameron's bit of paper, she thought, there are nasty doings here. Maybe some of the names on the paper were on *The Talbert*. She wondered. If so, that would make it a very risky ship indeed, with some of the seamen as … what? Traitors? Spies? Friendly towards the French? What was in it for them, she asked herself, as she stared round the men being got ready to embark.

Setton was moving amongst them now, looking closely at some, snapping at them, it seemed, and turning away from others.

The men watched him sullenly. Some of them were shackled, standing in a crowd, and a few fierce-looking sailors hemmed them in. In the middle, his red head up, his eyes glaring from beneath his bushy brows, was Harry. Beside him stood Jock, sullen, looking with a fixed stare at Setton.

Mary wriggled free of the restraining hands and moved up slowly. She moved round so that Setton had his back to her.

She made a small sound. A gasp.

Harry looked up, his eyes widened, jaw dropped. He stared at her, then looked down, shook his head and looked up again. This time there was some comprehension in his gaze, a belief that yes, there she was, Mary, his wife, in London, with him. Unbelievable but true. He made a small sign with his hands, one they used to use as youngsters – a sign which meant, 'Shh ... later ...'

She retreated, satisfied. Harry knew she was there. She'd done it! She'd got to him. And since she'd managed to come this far, now she knew for sure they would soon be together. She'd done it! Her eyes were full of tears, her lips trembling, her heart high. 'Harry!' she whispered. 'Harry, my man.'

She turned to Betty.

'I have to get him free, Betty, I have to ... how can I?'

'Doubt we can manage that!' Betty muttered. 'You just might have to go with him on the ship.'

Mary took a deep breath, and laid a hand on Bobby's arm.

'Bobby, I've got a ... an Exemption Certificate. Would that help?'

Bobby's eyebrows rose.

'An Exemption Certificate? For your man?'

'Well ...' Mary could not lie, but Bobby was pondering the matter.

'Might be a bit late in the day for that ... he's ower near boarding and they need the men.'

'But can I speak to somebody?'

'Bit late, lass, you can try but I doubt you'll find the right person.'

'Maybe I *should* go on the ship with him.

How will I get aboard? What do I say? And when?' She knew that during the long journey the question of boarding the ship had been churning in her brain. Go or not go? Board or stay on shore? Now it was decision time, and there was no doubt in her mind. She would go.

'I'll find out,' Bobby offered. He turned his sightless eyes towards the boat and walked off carefully stamping and swinging his stick rhythmically. Men moved aside to give him a clear passage.

While he was gone Betty said,

'It'll not be easy, Mistress. But if you're set on it, you'd best dress up as a man. Lots of the women do, it's easier that way. We can get you breeches, and a coat and shirts. But I say it again. It's not for the likes of you. You'll see and hear things you'd never dream of, sitting around in Fife.'

They heard Bobby's stick and turned.

'Ship sails on the evening tide. And no, your certificate is too late. But you've got time to get on board. And what you'll have to do is sign on as an 'idler', a lad who'll do anything he's asked.'

'Like?'

Betty grinned.

'Mess cook, surgeon's assistant, deck

scrubber.' But her face sobered quickly as she looked at Mary. Even unkempt grubby and torn clothing, she still looked too respectable to be on the ship as a scrubber.

But Mary was pleased.

'Sounds almost like home!' she giggled. Now that her goal had been reached, now that she'd seen Harry, she'd seen Jock, she felt light-hearted and safe. They'd see this thing through together.

The threesome turned back to stroll along the dockside. Mary kept her head down, not wanting to attract attention. Especially with Lieutenant Setton nearby. She was happy. She'd seen Harry.

'Can I get a message to his mother?' she wondered.

'Aye, I can do that for you,' Betty agreed. 'I'll send a note – if ... if, ah ...'

Mary understood. Betty couldn't read or write.

'Aye, I'll write it. Soon as I get back to Jem's.'

'Right! Back we go.' And Betty set off at a fast trot, leaving Bobby to make his own way.

CHAPTER SEVENTEEN

With Betty guiding her, it didn't take long to get back to the Limehouse inn. Betty grabbed her arm, and they moved fast along the streets, dodging in and out of strollers, in and out of the groups of sailors, jumping over coiled ropes, ignoring street sellers' cries, booth owners' blandishments.

'This way,' panted Betty.

'That's where I went wrong, went the other road,' gasped Mary.

'Slow down, slow down, slow down, ladies!' Jem stood in front of them.

'We've found him, we've found him. He's to be on *The Talbert*,' Mary stopped beside him. She put her arm through Betty's, drawing her friend into the conversation.

Jem pursed his lips, raised his eyebrows.

'So! *The Talbert*, eh? That's going to be very ... interesting.'

'How so, sir?' Mary was curious, needing to know more about Harry's ship, Harry's environment, and perhaps, even, her own immediate future.

Ewan Cameron appeared.

'So Harry's going to be on *The Talbert*?'

Mary eyed him frostily. Was he going to delay her again?

'Well, sir? what of it?'

He didn't answer directly. Instead, he inspected his fingernails.

'Did you just ... maybe ... happen to see Lieutenant Setton?' he inquired softly.

'Who's he?' asked Betty.

'Ah,' said Cameron. 'Another Scot?'

'From Edinbro.' Betty drew herself up proudly. 'And I'm a McGregor.'

'A fine warrior clan,' said Mr Cameron

politely.

Betty's face crumpled and her mouth quivered. She turned to Mary.

'And I'm a great example!' she said sarcastically.

Mary put her arm round her friend.

'You're doing well. Look how you've been helping me.'

Ewan Cameron watched them, a softened expression in his eyes. Jem coughed.

'We have little time to waste, mistresses, if we're going to ... erhm, help Mistress Watson meet her husband.' Jem moved off.

Mary looked up from comforting her friend.

'How to do it?' she wondered.

'Come inside, to the inn, ladies.' Mr Cameron turned away. 'And have something to eat.'

Mary and Betty could only follow where Mr Cameron pointed, into a parlour, and found Jem dusting chairs, setting them round a table.

'Food will be here presently, and a glass of ale?'

Mary sat down, tucking her skirts up from the grubby floor. She did want food, but her main aim was to discuss what to do about getting on the ship before it sailed. And how to use the Exemption Certificate, if she could get the chance. Bobby might think it was too late, but what if she could use it for all of them? For Harry, Jock and Archie Stott?

Betty stood beside her, unsure of what she should do.

'Pray be seated, Mistress.' Mr Cameron pulled out a chair beside Mary.

Mary leaned forward, catching Jem's eyes.

'My friend, my new friend, Betty, is from Scotland, like me.'

Jem frowned.

'How'd you do,' he said coldly, making his first acknowledgement of Betty's presence.

'It's a' right, said Betty softly. 'You're thinking am I one of them, one of the local prostitutes, and maybe I am. But I want to help Mistress Mary here.'

Jem was unrelenting and sharp.

'Can you prove that, Mistress?'

'No, no I canna, ehm, can't prove it, but I can tell you a few things you mightn't know. About *The Tarbert*.'

'There's something suspicious about the

ship, isn't there?' Mary demanded. 'I wanted to leave it to you. But now I need to know more. I mean to get on board and I want to know what am I getting into.'

Ewan Cameron leaned forward.

'Jem!' he commanded, 'a glass of toddy for us all, if you please.'

'Ale, if you please, sirs,' Mary was not a whisky-drinker. But Betty was. She nodded her thanks enthusiastically, eyes shining.

Jem set down a glass of ale in front of Mary and then poured out three glasses of toddy, setting them one in front of Betty, Cameron and himself. Betty downed hers quickly,

'Mistress,' began Cameron, 'there are things going on which none of us likes.'

He turned to Betty.

'Mistress, we three here are known to each other, but ...'

She broke in, holding up her right hand.

'You can trust me. I swear it. I swear by my home country, I swear by all that is Scottish and dear to me.'

Cameron kept his countenance.

'We cannot ask for more,' he said gravely.

But Mary caught a hint of a smile behind the words. She leaned forward in her turn.

'Betty helped me escape from Setton. She took me to the docks, showed me *The Talbert*, we found Harry ...' her voice trembled. 'She is my friend.'

'On that basis, then, Mistress,' said Mr Cameron, 'we will proceed.'

Was there a noise outside the door? A slight knock? A cough?

Jem got up, opened the door, and peered out. He turned and nodded.

'The food is here. I'll deal with it, sir.' Jem carried in a big tray, laden with pots. A waiter followed, with bowls and plates. He ignored the women but bowed slightly to Mr Cameron as he set them down on the table. Jem ladled some fine smelling meat into each bowl. Mary and Betty exchanged a glance. This was to be a good feast, by the smell of it. Jem handed the bowls round, and Mary reached forward for some bread. She broke it and stirred it into her bowl of stew. The glorious fragrance rose, almost numbing her mind. She chewed her stew-laden bread. When had she last eaten? Certainly whenever it was it had not been as delicious as this meal.

Mr Cameron leaned forward, lowering his

voice. He too was stirring his stew with his bread. And Betty likewise. But, thought Mary, back to business. Mr Cameron spoke quietly.

'We suspect Setton of smuggling, and he is also part of a group which is linked to France through the former Auld Alliance connections. Now we have evidence to arrest him. But if we leave him, and watch him, he may lead us to others, perhaps more important traitors. And *The Talbert* has been the main ship, maybe the headquarters of the conspirators. Most like, some of the press gang are also conspirators, and perhaps, just perhaps, one or two of the men they pressed, or pretended to press, are helping in some way.'

Could she ask questions? Mary decided to try.

'Sir, who do you mean by "we"?' She hesitated. 'Do you mean a group of your friends? Or mayhap something more official?'

Cameron nodded. Observant and shrewd, he thought, and careful. He gave her the best answer he could.

'I am not allowed to say, Mistress, it is something you will have to take on trust.' He tugged at his cravat.

'One more question, sir, if I may?'

He nodded.

'You are not wearing your sling now. Has your wound healed?'

She sounded concerned, and he smiled his appreciation of her care. 'It has healed sufficiently, Mistress, that I need no more support.'

She supped again, as did the others round the table. There seemed to be some unspoken agreement to eat and enjoy before discussing major business.

Finally the last spoonful had been supped, the last crust of bread eaten, and Mary at least was feeling considerably more at ease. So was Betty, leaning back on her chair, smiling and still licking her lips.

'Ahha, that was a fine meal.' Jem was clearly proud of it. He pushed forward their glasses of ale. 'Now, back to business.'

Mary nodded. She'd understood at least a hint of Setton's treachery in their previous discussions and through looking at the paper scrap, and the translation by Mr Cameron. Then she'd declared she wanted no part of it. But with Setton's seizing of her, his demands for the paper, and her sight of him at the docks, in his Royal Navy uniform, at the ship she needed to board, it looked as if she was involved whether she liked it or not.

Betty nodded as well.

'Mhhmm,' she said, 'we'll help.'

'We?' Mr Cameron raised his eyebrows.

'Me and my intended.' Betty's voice cracked slightly. 'He meets a lot of people around the docks, hears things. People think he's a fool because he's blind, but he's no fool! So, well, between us we know a few things.'

Cameron stared at her.

'We shall certainly need to get you and your ... intended ... along with us, Mistress Betty,' he said.

'Maybe we can tell you a few things,' Betty mumbled again.

Mary gazed down at the table and the empty bowls. What a peaceful quiet innocent life I lead she thought, up there in Fife, fishing, feeding folk, helping out, going to the kirk. While here ... here ... we're involved with – goodness knows what! She felt as if she'd lived a hundred years. The Mary Watson of Fife was not the Mary Watson of London.

Cameron touched her arm.

'Excuse me, Mistress, may we know your thoughts?'

Mary came back to earth.

'My ... my thoughts, sir? I fear they are not

worth the knowing.'

'Nevertheless …' Cameron murmured. She stiffened and drew back a little from the small group, creating a barrier of space between herself and the others. She sounded more punctilious, giving a warning of privacy not to be invaded.

'I do not wish to be ungracious, sir, but my thoughts were simply about home, and the innocent life we lead there. My thoughts here are that we are involved with great affairs of state and nation, of life and national safety. And I am afraid.'

'These are thoughts worth the knowing, Mistress,' said Cameron quietly. 'Yet, in spite of your fear, are you willing to help us?'

'Us, sir?' she asked again.

'I cannot tell you more, indeed I would not if I could – the less you know of who we are, the better. But I can tell you, we are British to the core, and much mislike those who consort with the enemy. We do not wish to see a French invasion of our shores.' Cameron sipped his ale and wiped his mouth. He continued, 'Nor do we wish that Scotland, broken free, should consort with France against England.'

'My only aim, sir, is to find my husband and free him.' She snapped out the words. Her eyes sparkled, her colour was heightened, her dress strained across the firm bosom, and she leaned forward, the better to emphasize her words. Cameron became even quieter.

'To free him, Mistress, will be difficult. Very difficult.'

'Yet I must ask how it is to be done. I have an Exemption Certificate.' She was still leaning towards him. He looked into her shining eyes and soft lips and stifled a sigh of regret. Lucky Harry, he thought.

'We can but try, Mistress. I shall be on the ship myself – perhaps I can have a word with the Captain.'

Betty muttered an oath. Mary turned to her, eyes flashing.

'Were it your man, Betty, you would be the same.'

'I would that, Mistress Mary, but there are things to be thought of, how to get a man off a ship ... can you do it when the Navy is just about to set sail and face the enemy? If you tried, and failed, then you'd never get on board yourself! Oh, Mistress, there are many, many things ...'

Jem nodded.

'She's in the right of it, Mistress.'

'What's to do, then? If I cannot free him –

maybe I can join him?   On the ship? I've had thoughts of maybe nursing, helping.'

There was such resolution in her voice that the men stared at her. Betty shook her head.

'I still think thon ships, Mistress Mary, are not the place for you.'

Mr Cameron thoughtfully tapped his fingers on the table. The sound was like a drum roll, a call to action.

'Officers' wives on board, Mistress, are there by permission of the captain. And yes, they nurse and mend amongst the officers.'

Jem and Cameron exchanged glances.

'But Harry Watson will not be an officer,' Jem murmured.

'It will be a crowded scene, Mistress,' Cameron continued. 'Noisy, smelly, dirty, and ...' he wondered whether he should suggest that seamen were not always – perhaps 'respectful,' would be a good word to use. He tried it. 'Seamen, Mistress, are not always respectful to a woman.'

'But I would be with Harry, sir,' Mary said quietly.

'He would have his work to do. He could not always protect you.'

'But it is worth considering, getting on board,' said Jem.

'Never!' said Betty. 'Think again! Never at all. A gently-born woman like my friend here, on board the ship? No.' In spite of her predicament, Mary smiled to hear herself described as 'gently-born'. Betty saw the smile and guessed the reason. 'You're not a street woman, Mistress, nor have you seen the insides of the slums here, the dirt, the stench, the disease. You've come from the fresh air and freedom of the Kingdom of Fife.'

'Yet I know hard work as many women may not know it,' Mary put in. 'I know care of the sick, the dying, I know the method of cooking cheap food to make it nourishing and edible, I know the need for cleanliness. I can make a bed quickly, I can run, I can do the bidding of others ...'

Mr Cameron took a turn about the room, pulling at his chin.

'There is much in what Mistress McGregor says, Mistress Watson. But it may be the only way to help your Harry ... and ...' His eyes were hooded, as he stared at her. Would she be of help in the capture of a traitor? Could he ask this of a young woman? Her courage was beyond doubt, she had contacts on board the ship, her husband and his friend. No doubt but there would be support from this threesome.

His stare discomfited Mary and she raised a hand to break the look. Betty stared at him. Her eyes were cold as she snapped at the two men.

'To help you, you mean.'

Mr Cameron made up his mind.

'I do not deny it, Mistress McGregor, but we are in sore need. Our country is in sore need.'

'What is it you would have me do?' Mary asked.

'Go on board. Keep in touch with the others. Watch for Setton, who will be on *The Talbert*, and report to me. I shall be there also.'

'What about the Exemption Certificate, sir? When can we use that? It may be that I do not go on board if Harry is freed.'

Cameron frowned.

'I can try, but it should have been presented before we reached this point, Mistress. It is for landsmen to remain on land.' She started to speak but he held up his hand. 'It may be that we can use it to get him off after this voyage. Rather than remain on board for five years as is usual for pressed men. Keep it safe – though even if it will work for one, it will not work for both the men you seek.'

She sighed. So there was to be no reprieve yet.

'And Archie Stott, too, sir,' she added, hoping that might prick his conscience, but Mr Cameron only shrugged.

'I have not yet found him.'

CHAPTER EIGHTEEN

So it was back to that, was it? On board? Give up ideas of getting Harry exempt immediately. Too late, Cameron and Bobby both said. But maybe that was only because Cameron wanted Harry's and her own help. On board but for *their* purposes, not her own of being with Harry and helping him get free. And helping Jock, too. Jeannie must be worried sick, and her with a bairn to come.

How was it to happen? The debate raged between Betty and Jem over dressing as a man or sneaking on as a woman. Mary thought her preference would be for a disguise. There would be other women there, she was sure, but if, if, she were to try to get close to Harry, maybe it was better to be disguised.

It was agreed eventually. Men's clothing to be worn. Jem went off to look out suitable sailor's clothing.

'As an idler, Mistress, that's what you'll be.

A sailor who moves round the ship, doing what he's told. And I'll put it in your room, Mistress, and I'll get something for you to hide your bawbees in.'

'I'll owe you …'

'No. It's all taken care of.'

'Who by?' Mary wondered. Cameron? Unknown groups? It made her nervous: she liked to be open and direct and this secretive stuff worried her.

Betty tugged her sleeve.

'It's time,' she whispered.

Mary took a deep breath. She *would* dress up as a man. She *would* make it her business to be with Harry, and if anything else came of it, like what Cameron had suggested, that would be a bonus.

Her knees were shaking so much that she thought her clothes would show the trembling.

'I could bide here.' A last misgiving. 'I don't have to put myself through this.' But she thought of Harry. He had been forced to go. And there was nothing she wanted in life more than to be with him, her man. They would share whatever came to them.

It was time to get dressed. With Betty beside her, she turned and threaded her way through the old inn, from a well-hidden door in her bedroom, along a narrow passageway, and into another room.

'Come on!' said Betty again. She put a comforting arm around Mary's shoulders. 'It's a big adventure, so it is. Better than sticking around here. Wish I was comin' with you.'

She led the way into the bedroom. A pair of clean trousers lay on the bed, two shirts, and a neat coat with black buttons.

Mary picked up the trousers.

'Hurry! Come on, hurry!'

Mary untied the strings of her skirt first. Then she pushed her legs into the trousers.

'Hope no one back in Fife ever sees me like this.' She stroked the sailcloth lightly. 'They're rough!' She wriggled into the trouser legs, pulled them up round her waist, and tied them as tightly as she could. The shirt came next, then she shrugged into the canvas coat and fastened it.

'Hair!' Betty said abruptly. 'Hair, a quick trim.' She sliced off some of Mary's long locks. 'Now I'll braid it in a tail. Quick now.'

Someone knocked at the door and pushed it open.

Both women stood still, fearful, until Jem's head poked round the door.

'Ready?'

'Aye, just about.' Mary touched the braid Betty had made. She moved awkwardly in her unaccustomed trousers. 'Aah! They're rough! I must have something between them and my skin.' She ducked back to the bed and grabbed her old petticoat. 'Quick, Betty, help me cut this down the middle.' The two women slid a knife up the material back and front, splitting it into two.

'I haven't got time to stitch it up, but I must just put it on like it is.' Jem turned his back as Mary wriggled free of her trousers and slid into her slit up petticoat. She wrapped it round her legs, and pulled on the trousers again, making sure that the soft cloth was between her tender skin and the roughness of the breeches. 'That's better! Thank goodness I remembered my petticoat. I'd have been ripped to pieces with that stuff.' She tried to laugh as she moved around, checking her shape in the mirror. Her shirt and seaman's jacket gave her a straighter outline, hiding her breasts. The wide trousers were tidy, showing no signs of the bulky petticoat beneath. She heaved her own clothes into a bag Jem had given her. He had offered to look after her things.

'Until you're both back, safe and sound.' He smiled at her as he took the bag. But his eyes had an anxious look.

'Right! Give me my sailor hat!' And with

that on her head, she opened the door.

Mr Cameron stood waiting.

'A fine sailor, Mistress.' He too made a fine sailor, powerful in the uniform of a lieutenant, with a large cocked hat under his arm. He saluted her.

'I shall be with you on board *The Talbert*, Mistress. You must look on me as a friend in need, and should you learn anything you must let me know at once. We will arrange discreet meeting places where any information can be passed on immediately.'

She touched her forelock.

'Aye aye, sir!'

He laughed.

'Well done, Mistress.'

Jem appeared at Cameron's elbow.

'Good luck, both of you. And, Mistress, if you get back … I mean *when* you get back … you can command a room here.'

'Thank you.' She was surprised and touched by his generosity and by a glistening in his eyes, teary and affectionate.

Mary and Betty left the tavern, heads held high, Betty holding Mary's arm in a fine show of affection. They marched down the rough path towards the docks. The women in the doorways laughed at them and waved.

'Good luck!' they shouted. 'Good luck. God go with you.'

Mary managed a wave in return but was caught up in the horrors of memory, being grabbed, bruised, subtle blows, pokes and punches, being helpless, being attacked. She thought she would never forget that time, not as long as she lived. And she wondered fearfully what lay ahead? She trudged along the docks with Betty, right to the end. There was the boat for *The Talbert*, and men were boarding her.

Betty gave her a hug.

'On you go. Good luck!' The words seemed sparse, but the warm hug and the tears on Betty's cheeks showed the depth of her feelings.

Mary gripped her hand. No last-minute changes, she thought. Just keep going! She was caught up in a group of tars, some clean, some dirty and dishevelled, some whistling, some groaning, 'Here we go again.' She thought someone tapped her on the shoulder, and she turned. But it wasn't Harry, nor was it Jock, though she thought she spotted one or two other pressed Fifers in the group. But no one recognised her, and she failed to identify anyone who had tapped her.

Singing, whistling, spitting, grumbling, the group reached *The Talbert*'s boat. Among this rough crew, Mary was pushed on to the gangplank where she was jostled up to the boat along with a line of other seamen. The beating of the drums made a sinister undertone to the men marching on board.

'Name!'

'Harry Watson, sir!' Mary snapped. It was the only name she could think of.

'We've got one Harry Watson already.' The midshipman glared at her.

'I'm another one, sir!' Mary was quick to reply.

'Hmm,' and the name was put down. 'Harry Watson Two. Experience?'

'None, sir!'

'Ah, hmm. An idler, for the galley and the surgeon's quarters. On you go!'

It seemed to take only seconds for the boat to reach the towering sides of The Talbert, out on the open water. Rope ladders dangled over the side, and Mary managed to scramble up the nearest one with the others from the boat. The deck above was busy.

'Where now?' muttered Mary to herself. A man overhearing her pointed to a flight of steps.

'Down below.'

Clutching her small pack, she followed other men to the steep steps inside down to the hold. It was dark, smelly and crowded already, men, women and even children moving around in a perpetual gloom and stench. The ship's movement under her feet made her feel unsteady, and she spread her feet to get better balance.

The bosun's mate was bellowing orders.

'Clear out, women and children. Men! On deck!'

She groaned.

'I've just come down.'

'Up on deck. Up we go.' Men and boys ran past Mary, and she joined in the rush up to the upper gun deck. She squirmed through the throng as they lined up. Line by line, she checked to try to find Harry.

At last! After staring around at more than fifty men she spotted his red head, near the front of the line! He was standing with Jock. Amidst grunts and curses, and elbows in her ribs, hands gripping her to push her aside, she wriggled and pushed and shoved until she was near them. Harry's jaw dropped and his eyes popped. Jock turned round, and she whispered out of the side of her mouth.

'Psst, Harry! Harry! It's me!'

'Whaaat? Whaaat?' he turned his head, disbelieving.

'FACE FRONT!' the order was barked out.

The men formed lines and faced the bosun's mate. Orders to come, she thought, and faced front with the rest. But with Harry beside her, even these circumstances could not unnerve her. Well, maybe not completely!

'What are you doin' here?' Harry whispered back.

"NO TALKING IN THE RANKS!'

Harry forced his eyes forward, but he had another quick peek.

Orders came thick and fast. Mary found herself in a Mess group of enlisted men with both Harry and Jock.

'Down below decks!' bellowed the bosun's mate.

'Come on!' Harry grabbed her arm. 'Down to get our hammock space.'

As an enlisted seaman, Mary was entitled to a hammock for herself. Had she remained as a woman, she would have had to share her husband's hammock – and at fourteen inches of space, that was a cramped area. However, she managed to get the hammock space next to Harry and hang up her hammock, turning it on a nail.

'What are you doin' here?' he demanded again, not sure whether to be furious with her, or happy to see her. Bit of both, she thought!

'Couldna let you go without me,' she whispered back.

Then she turned to Jock, on Harry's other side, so that both men could hear her. 'We need to think too of an Archie Stott, a youngster frae Edinburgh, who was pressed a wee while ago. And, Jock, I need to tell you that Jeannie's doin' well, Jock, she's thinkin' of you.'

Was this the time to pass over the ring? Mary started fumbling for it in her pockets, but another shout from the bosun's mate had her running back up to the deck.

CHAPTER NINETEEN

Once back in the line-up, she stood next to Harry, facing forwards again, shoulders back, back rigid, trying not to grin at his stunned expression. He copied her, but managed to mutter,

'What's goin' on?'

'Tell you later.'

'You make a grand young man … I'm real happy to see you,' he murmured, his mouth lifting in a smile.

'No talking in the ranks!' The bosun's mate from the gangplank was standing in front of the men. 'Like it or not, you're all a blue in the Andrew! Meaning?' – and he turned to a nearby sailor.

'You're in the Royal Navy now, sir!' snapped the sailor.

'And why Blue and Andrew?'

The sailor was silent.

'I'll tell you!' barked the bosun's mate. 'A

'blue' is a soldier's name for a sailor! And 'the Andrew' is because one Andrew Miller pressed so many men that he said this isn't the Royal Navy, it's my navy.'

A few men laughed; most were silent. The bosun's mate eyed them with disgust. 'You need to get ready for the sea. And for a battle.' He glared again. 'Now for your duties.'

'You, you and you – in the first Mess.' He pointed to several men. 'And you.' He turned to Mary. 'Watson 2! Um, no experience …' Mary held her breath. She knew something of fishing boats, but nothing of these great sailing ships with their massive decks, their guns, and their big cabins. 'You're in that Mess, too, and you can start by doing duty as Mess Cook for a few days.'

'Aye, aye, sir!' Mary replied, saluting, palm inward as the other did.

'Right! After that the surgeon'll need help. Report to Mr Graham this day week.'

'Aye, aye, sir!' Mary deepened her voice to a growl. She saluted again.

The mess deck was situated on the lower gun deck. She squeezed down the narrow stairway that Harry pointed out, to the cramped lower deck. Then she squeezed through the innumerable seamen, sickened by the sheer number of men and the press of them against her. The stink of unwashed bodies persisted in her nostrils. There was no time to sit and reflect, there was no time to look round, and there was no chance now of changing her mind. This was no blithe adventure with Harry that she'd imagined. This was real fighting stuff and she was seen as a man and had to play her part. Otherwise … she wondered what would happen to her? Walk the plank? Held down in irons? All the stories of naval cruelty came back to haunt her. She had that gnawing gut feeling of constant anxiety and fear.

The trousers were still rough against her skin, even through her petticoat. They were too tight across her hips, and she disliked the feeling of her hips being visible in walking and movement. Moving in skirts was different from moving in trousers. Did men walk differently? Surreptitiously she checked how the men around her were walking. Where was Harry? She could ask him how she looked and what she should do.

'I was too excited to get here,' she reflected inwardly. 'I didn't think of what it would be like.' Harry might suffer too. What had she done? Wouldn't it have been better to have remained on shore?

She squeezed along the narrow passageway, the press of the crowd pushing her against the wall, the stench of the unwashed bodies would linger for ever in her nostrils, she thought. One body pressed harder against her than any others, pushing her back against the cabin wall. Breathlessly she looked up. The grim face of Setton looked down on her. Like Mr Cameron, he was in the uniform of a lieutenant. His jaw dropped, and his eyes widened.

'Ahha, Mistress … so you are *here* … I wonder, now. I wonder very much …'

But in a moment even he was pushed on by a crowd of men behind him, sliding past, moving along, trying to get to the mess deck. But as he moved on, he looked over his shoulder.

'I'll be watching out for you,' he hissed back at her. It didn't sound a kindly promise.

She shuddered. A touch on her shoulder made her turn. Harry was behind her, his eyes anxious, his lips gripped tightly together.

'You look fine, lass, a real man. Keep it up.'

'In trousers?'

'Aye, you're doin' fine.'

Jock was beside him, eyes swivelling towards Setton.

'Watch out for that one, mistress. He's up to no good.'

They were all pushed along by the crowd

behind them. She tried to keep up with Harry, inching along the deck, still apprehensive, still with the churning feelings of anxiety. Even with Harry there, and the friendly Jock, she felt isolated in this seething mass of men, unsure of how to speak, what to do, where to go. Even the privies, she thought. How was she going to manage? What was she going to do, why hadn't she thought further ahead? She was endangering Harry as well as herself. She tugged at her neckcloth, disarranging its careful folds.

'Sling yer hammocks here!' A sailor was directing them into the lower gun deck. 'Keep yer pitch right, sling yer hammock when you need to sleep, you're not on watch or working.'

There's not enough room, Mary protested silently. She hooked up the hammock in the place she and Harry had chosen earlier, and lashed it to two pillars.

'Just practisin',' she said to Harry as he squeezed in next to her to check the hammocks. Jock slung his hammock next to them. 'Friends,' he breathed. 'A bit o' home.'

'This way we can be a bit more together,' Harry said to her, his hands lightly brushing her sleeve.

'We need a good talk.' She pulled her hammock as straight as she could and moved aside.

He grinned agreement, eyes crinkling at the corners. But already she was being summoned.

'This way to the galley!' a sailor bellowed along the line of men.

She lined up in the galley with other mess cooks. The cook, Ol' Pegleg by name, she learned, was himself stoking the galley stoves, arranging the pots. He moved round very quickly on his one good, and one wooden leg.

'Lookee 'ere. This 'ere is wot you use for cooking.' And he lifted up different pans. 'But first you gets the stores, from down below, then you prepares them, then you bring the stuff to me, and then I cooks them, and then you serves them up.'

'Eh? What?' came a chorus from the new mess cooks, including Mary.

'Ain't you never been to sea afore?' bellowed the cook. 'You calls me "sir". Got it?'

'Aye, aye, sir,' they chorused, and Mary touched her forelock.

'Sright, 'sright, you keep to that and we'll get on all right. Now!' he barked suddenly. 'Wot you has to do is this 'ere.' And he leaned against the big stove. 'You looks up 'ere – see?' and he pointed. '*If* you can read – which I make doubt of – you see wot we're a-goin' to 'ave to eat on each day. Today, now, it being a Tuesday, we 'ave salt beef. *You* goes and gets it – down in the 'old.'

And the instructions continued until Mary was dizzy with information.

'How much do we carry? Do we have to cut it up?' someone asked.

Cookie struck his forehead.

'Oh my lawd,' he moaned, 'where'd you come from?' He darted to the galley door, moving fast for such a bulky man with a wooden leg. 'Oy, Jenkins, come 'ere, come 'ere.'

A boy, maybe eleven, came running in.

'Aye, sir?'

'Take these 'ere new mess cooks down the 'old and show 'em a few things. Right?'

'Aye, aye, sir. You come alonga me,' said Jenkins cheerfully, and led the way down to the hold.

Later that night, after her first two efforts as mess assistant, Mary stood by the taffrail, watching the stars come out. The ship was dipping and swaying. Harry slipped in beside her. She gave a quick look round. No one in sight, but she pulled him back into the shadows of the main cabin. He hugged her and she flung her arms round his neck, pulling him even closer.

'We'll have to be very careful,' he said, touching her hair. She felt ashamed of it, short and tied back like that.

'D'you know, I didn't even feel us leave,' she said. 'I was so busy running up and down with cleaning the vegetables and taking them up with the meat, bread, biscuits, I didn't notice …' She cradled his face between her hands, smoothing the rough cheeks with long gentle fingers.

'Me neither,' confessed Harry. 'And I'm like to drop now. But before we turn in, I want to know … how's things back home, how did you get here, and … and …'

'How are we going to get back? And we need to get Jock back too.' Mary finished his sentence for him. 'Here's a quick tale. Grannie crying a lot, your mother just getting on with things, Jeannie upset. Mistress Wood said maybe I could be a nurse. And I got the stagecoach down and there was a Mr Cameron on as well and there's more to tell you… but … Harry,' and she looked round to see who might have come into earshot. She could see no one, but even so she lowered her voice still further. 'Harry, I'm worried. Lieutenant Setton!'

Harry groaned.

'Not him! He was in charge of the press gang! He's bad, a real bad yin. The men with him speak a bit o' the Auld Alliance.'

'Aye, he's for France! I pushed his horse off me in Sillery and he kept on pushing it back at me, with the spurs an' all, and I just kept pushing against him, grabbed his coat to try and pull him off his horse. And a bit of paper came away in my hand. Must've been important because he chased me in Sillery and to Edinburgh and London. The bit of paper fitted in with another bit of paper that Mr Cameron had, that shows he's in the pay of the French.' The quick version. She wanted to get the message to Harry that Setton was dangerous.

'So he could be … a spy?' She could barely catch his words.

'Maybe. He's got it in for me, anyway.'

Harry gritted his teeth.

'Not while I'm around,' he muttered.

Not for worlds would she have admitted to Harry how she'd been treated and how terrified she was of Lieutenant Setton. As a lieutenant he'd have all the power, and she agonized over possible consequences. Revealing her as a woman? Locked in irons? Trouble for Harry?

Eight bells sounded.

'Come on,' he said, 'time to turn in.'

Down below they squeezed along the rows

of hammocks until they found their own. But Harry's mind was still on Setton.

'Aye, there's somethin' goin' on there.' He frowned. 'Jock's on to him, as well. And there's more. Some on the ship we was on were awful pally with him.'

'Mr Cameron's here too, though. We can tell him if we need to, but what'll I do if I meet Setton again?' She was careful to keep too much anxiety out of her voice.

'Mm. Be careful. He's an officer. But a few of us have watched him, from Fife to London.' Harry grinned. 'He thinks we're stupid!'

Mary grinned too. Nothing stupid about the Fifers.

'And Jock heard him speaking – it sounded like French – to someone. Not that we could understand what he was saying. And we couldna see the other bloke.'

'Doesna have to mean anything. Or it could be something for our side.'

'So it could. I'll have to think about this, lass. Best have a sleep. We'll catch up on news later.' He slid into his own hammock, and Mary struggled into hers.

They were together at last!

CHAPTER TWENTY

The next few days were busier than Mary ever imagined could happen. Six bells meant a seven o'clock start for the crew to breakfast and work. A brown-haired lad with a familiar look to him was first cook – Mary was to assist him.

'I'm Stott, Watson: dinna worry, you'll soon catch on to it.'

Stott! Could it be?

She turned in the tiny space of the galley. True, this was Archie, as like his father as could be.

'Archie Stott? Frae Leith?'

'Aye, that's me.' He frowned. 'Do I know you?'

She shook her head.

'No. I bided with your Ma and Pa, they're fair worried.'

'Aye, it wasna easy in the beginning. There

was a lot to learn, and I was awful feart. But I'm a Scot, an' we aye win through.'

Mary nodded. That was similar to her own philosophy.

Archie continued,

'I'll get them a letter soon as I can. It's no' that easy to get word to folks.' And with that, he picked up the porridge oats to cook.

As mess assistant cook for the first week, she was required to be in the galley earlier to collect the food for her mess for the day. She began to enjoy the routine of going to the hold, checking the stores in their casks embedded in shingle to keep them steady. Then a word to the few bewildered pigs and cows on board, securely penned in, in what she learned was called 'the manger'. Then collecting food for breakfast and back up to the galley.

At the galley she helped to prepare the food, passed it to the cook, and then took the cooked food to her mess. Unlike some of her shipmates, she didn't suffer from seasickness. Her experiences in Fife had accustomed her to the movement of the sea. And she had no difficulty in eating, either, much to the disgust of her messmates.

The meat was pickled in salt. The water was fresh but would soon become green and undrinkable, she was told.

'We drink beer,' Jenkins told her on her first duty.

'Beer? Nothing else?'

He shook his head. 'Some ale, but not much.'

She was horror-struck.

'I don't like beer!'

'You 'ave to. Or wine, if there's any.'

The biscuits were becoming harder, but at least the vegetables were still fresh and fair by the end of the first week, thought Mary, and the oatmeal was still fresh and untouched by weevils or rats.

Archie told her,

'We lower the table, see?' And he pointed to the ropes. He laughed. 'I'll tell Ma and Da I'm fine! And this is a great life! The real stuff. I'm goin' to be a real sailor.'

The men had lowered the mess table, hanging by ropes from the rafters, and were sitting banging on it with their bowls. It swayed from side to side.

'Hold it,' she ordered. 'Here's the porridge.' She slid the pot on to the table and seized the ladle. Some of the men looked at her curiously. Was her voice too high? If she were challenged, she could say that she was but young, like Jenkins.

Harry got up.

'I'll get the grog.'

Jenkins sat down on the biscuit barrel at the end of the table.

'I'm powder monkey this week, I get to sit 'ere.' He picked up his wooden bowl and helped himself to a fill of porridge. 'Great! I'm hungry!'

She ladled out more bowlfuls.

'I'm on my last morning on the Mess here. I'm on to help the surgeon from tomorrow,' she told her messmates. 'I'll join you when I can.'

'You'll be kept busy.'

'Aye, that I will.' She gave the toast they always gave at mealtimes. 'Confusion to Boney!' Then she grinned and settled down to eat. Her next work would be interesting, and she wouldn't miss the bawdy talk and the raucous aggression of her messmates. She scraped her bowl clean and moved out into the gangway. 'I'm off! I'm supposed to be cleaning a bit of deck now.'

She sped back to the poop deck where she found the small sandstone scrubber called 'holystone' which she was bidden to scrub into cracks and crevices, where the larger scrubber couldn't go. The usual line of deck scrubbers was in front of her, moving their stones along the deck at an even pace. She slid behind them, rolled up her trousers almost to the knees with the tails of her petticoat well hidden, and got down to scrub into the crevices of the deck.

She was on her knees, scrubbing at the corner of the deck where the captain's cabin was, when a foot stood on her holystone, just missing her hand. Startled she looked up, expecting Harry.

It was Setton, cocked hat under his arm. He leered down at her, exposing a mouthful of strong white teeth, reminding her of a fox that lived in Sillery. He bent over her. She rubbed her eyes to banish the image.

'I know not what game you're playing, Mistress, but you might make it worth my while to keep my mouth shut.'

Mary scrambled to her feet, automatically dusting her knees. He laughed.

'Mistress, I salute you, you are a marvel. Charming woman first, keeping her clothes clean and tidy, and devoted wife too. I envy him. Who is he?'

She caught her breath. So he would try to find out about Harry, would he? And threaten them both? Her imagination had been at work in the past few days, ever since she had seen Setton was on board.

'Sir,' she began, 'I crave a boon. I'm here to be with my man. No other reason, but that we're wed, and we've made our promises. I crave that you leave us alone.'

Setton's voice purred.

'But Mistress, I can help you and your man. If I did but know who he was.' His hand slid up her forearm and he grasped it in a twist.

She gritted her teeth.

'You traitor!' thought Mary, 'I'll jump overboard before I tell you.'

'Mr Setton!' A shout came from the fo'c'sle. 'Here, sir! Here, I say. You're wanted. The captain wants a word.'

He took his hand off her arm, turned about, but twisted his head back to look at her.

'Don't forget, Mistress. I never do.' Menacing words.

'What did he want?' Harry stood beside her, puffing from his run up the staircase.

'To know who you are. Threatening us.'

He nodded and turned to the riggings, behind Jock, in line with a number of others. She watched, hand at her mouth, as the group were told,

'Get up there. Up to the top!'

Her gaze flickered across the men then up to the top of the rigging. Up there! Harry caught the lowest spar and swung himself easily upwards. She stared as he climbed, the first of them to move up.

'Wocha lookin' at? Be your turn next if you don't get crackin'.' The bosun's mate stood over her.

'Aye, aye, sir.' Those were the safest words, she thought.

She went back to her scrubbing, her spirits leaden, her heart in her mouth. What could Setton want with her and Harry? He might want the paper, but she no longer had it. How could she convince Setton of that, though?

She continued scrubbing hard, thinking as she did so, how she could best see Harry by himself.

Another foot stood in her way. Harry! Back again! She looked up gladly.

Ewan Cameron stood there, in the immaculate uniform of a lieutenant, his cocked hat shading his face, his boots shining, and a sword swinging at his hip.

'Eh … eh …' stuttered Mary. 'I mean … sir …' She stood up and saluted quickly.

He waved away her stammering.

'Just making sure all is well, Master Watson. Have you met our friend yet?'

'Aye, yes, I have – sort of. I mean … aye, aye, sir,' she stammered again.

He ignored the stammer and lowered his voice.

'We think he is under orders, Master Watson, to send news of the movement of the fleet to the French, and to create an uprising. To take Nelson's attention away from the French.'

She stared.

'How? Why?'

'That, as yet, we can only suspect. Perhaps discreet signals from on board. We must watch carefully. Can we rely on you and your husband?'

'Aye, aye, sir. And there's Jock.' Conscious of other sailors moving around, Mary deepened her voice again.

'I'd like to meet them both. We will want exact reports wherever possible of our friend's doings. And we need to know, if possible, who his contacts are. Who does he talk to? And should you see anything suspicious at all, I want you to report it to me as soon as ever you can.'

'How shall we find you, sir?'

'Can we try to meet on this part of the upper gun deck? At, say, eight bells every evening?'

She looked round her. The deck had guns along both sides. There were small boats on cradles over the open space in the middle. There were men by the guns, men by the boat, men cleaning the deck. It was an ideal place to meet since it was so open. Anyone watching would think that an officer was ordering a couple of seamen to undertake some tasks.

She nodded.

'We can but try, sir.'

She palmed her forehead. He nodded, half-closed one eye, and moved away.

'What did he want?' Harry was back, rubbing his hands, scarred and tarred from the ropes.

'Tell you later,' she hissed back and bent further over her scrubbing, giving the holystone one last push into the corners.

When she got up from her knees, rolled down her trousers again, and picked up her gritty stone, shaking flakes off it into a cloth she carried, Harry had moved off.

'So that's the man, is it?' Setton's voice sounded gritty in her ear.

'I've just been watchin' them climb the rigging,' Mary said. 'I don't know who that was.' She moved away, taking her holystone scrubber with her.

CHAPTER TWENTY-ONE

A rough awakening at six bells had Mary tumbling out of her hammock. She had slept surprisingly well, despite the information from Mr Cameron and the talk with Setton, not to mention the discomfort of a hammock, and the crowding and stench of the lower decks. Today she hoped she'd get a chance to talk further with Harry. His hammock next to her was rolled up. She thought he might be on watch.

'Up you get, my hearties!' came the yell from the doorway. This was the day she was to start as surgeon's apprentice. A loblolly boy, she thought. She longed for water to wash her face, to waken her up, she longed for a brush to run through her hair, and she longed, above all, to get out of her trousers.

'Come on, get moving!' A kick aimed at her made her skip out of the way. 'Up to the mess.'

Jenkins was on mess cook duties and the table was laid and ready with oatmeal breakfast, biscuits and some salt beef. She turned down the beef, but took the thick glutinous oatmeal. There was a drop or two of fresh milk. Jenkins winked at her as he gave her the jug. He must have siphoned it off some of the officers' rations, she thought. She wondered how long the fresh milk would last, how long the cows would continue to give milk. Jenkins must have seen her surprise.

'Got that special like,' he said. 'The old cow's giving off milk this morning, and I went and got some.'

'Thanks. Thank you.' She wiped her mouth and escaped from the table before Harry got there. If she could catch him as he came off watch, and before his breakfast, she might be able to give him some of her news, let alone seeing him, touching him, maybe even time and space for a quick hug. Maybe best not to hug, though, she thought. What would the other men think? But she longed for his touch, to bury her face in his shoulder, to smell what she called to herself 'Fife' in his clothing and on his skin. Harry meant home, and more than that, safety, security, someone to trust and share with and above all, a sense of belonging.

This morning, however, she was disappointed. No Harry appeared on the deck.

'He's aloft, Mistress.' Jock put his hand to his mouth. 'Sorry!'

Mary looked round. No one in sight, thank goodness.

'Be careful!' she hissed at him.

Unwillingly, she turned away. Back to work, she thought, get on with it. And she started what she called her 'seaman's run', a jogtrot slanted to the movement of the ship, to get her quickly along the deck. At least this was work near her own heart, the tending and healing of the sick.

Breathlessly she reached the orlop deck, climbing backwards down the open stairs.

'Come in.' Graham had a gruff voice. 'Ah yes, you're my latest loblolly boy. Hope you're a good one. Not squeamish, are you?' The boys in the orlop turned to stare at her, the low lighting masking some of the possibly telltale features of her womanhood.

She gazed around. Surgeon Graham was standing by an open box, with its first tray full of knives, curved needles and thread, or so it seemed to her.

'No, no, I don't think so, sir.'

'Good! Because we have to begin with an amputation. Gun fell on Mr Midshipman Lively and crushed his lower left arm. It has to come off at the elbow. So we're gathering everything we need to do the job on deck.'

Soon she was laden with buckets and boxes, and staggering up on deck with the other boys.

'Prepare the area,' Graham barked at them. She looked round for a table. He nudged her and pointed to a big chair. 'That's it, for now at least. When battle commences, then we move our actions down to the orlop deck – no light and precious little room, but at least we're below the waterline.'

One of the other boys was arranging buckets near the chair. Another was crashing open doors, pulling out a large sheet from a store lying on the deck.

'Clean the chair, spread a sheet on it, sand on the floor to catch the blood, get the sponges. And water.'

Water? Where to get water? But a bucket of boiling water already stood near the entrance.

'Boiling water,' Graham confirmed, 'and plunge the knife into it.'

'Why, sir?' Mary was spreading a sheet

over the chair, as a boy ladled sand from another bucket to cover the deck.

'Nelson says a cold knife is more … unpleasant, shall we say? than a warm knife. And I agree with him.'

She bit her lip. This was going to take a lot of learning on her part.

'There should be a leather strap in that box by your feet,' Graham called to her.

'This it, sir?' She held up a thick leather strip.

'That's it. It's a gag, he bites on it when the pain is too much.' She wanted to ask more questions, he saw, and he nodded permission.

'Do you give him laudanum, sir?'

'Forget the sir after every comment, if you please!' She nodded. 'Laudanum? I might prescribe it afterwards. Nor do I give spirits before the operation, since that may cause the patient to become unruly. There is a cordial of spirits and fruit juice to be given afterwards, which helps his recovery.'

Mary looked round the surgical area: all seemed to be in order, she thought, knives at the ready, towels to catch more blood.

'Right, all ready?' Graham looked around. 'More towels, please, there will be a lot of blood.

And another bucket of sand in case there's even more spillage of blood than we anticipate.'

'And to hinder the rats,' muttered one boy.

'Rats?' Mary hissed at him. He nodded and she made a disgusted face.

She scooped more sand from sacks on the deck, and scattered it beside the operating table.

'Good! Well done! Bring him over.'

The young midshipman was seated nearby, clutching at his injured arm. Mary went over to him.

'Come and sit over here now.'

The man looked up at her, sweating, his face grimed with dust, his mouth gritted against the pain.

'Is it … time?'

She nodded, and placed her hand on his good shoulder.

'Aye. We will do our best for you.' Privately she hoped it was true.

He winced and grimaced and suppressed a groan as he got to his feet, his left arm supported in his right hand.

'Take off his coat,' said the surgeon.

'Aaaargh!' The yell of pain stopped her trying to ease the coat off.

'Cut it, cut it!' Graham snapped. She picked up a big knife and slit through the fabric, sliding the left sleeve off quickly. The arm was hanging by a thread. Stuck in the shattered elbow were threads of cloth, and bits of bone. She turned away, struggling not to vomit. Blood soaked the makeshift bandages she'd dislodged when taking off the sleeve. Her hands were spattered with blood, her clothes had spots on them.

'Sit down!' Graham barked.

The officer clutched his injured arm, and leaned on the loblolly boys, as they tried to walk him over to the big chair. He whimpered and groaned as his arm was jolted by the walking. With a shudder, he sat down, his eyes closed, his mouth gripped tightly.

Mary looked down with pity. His eyes were open, but not seeing her or anyone else. He stared beyond to the ship's railing and the sea beyond, as if seeking escape.

'Right. Hold him.' The surgeon tied a tourniquet on the arm just above the elbow.

She took her place just behind the chair and held the shoulder firmly.

'Not like that. Press down hard! Harder! So that he can't move and mess up my work.'

She gulped. The blood was oozing faster now, trickling down into the sawdust and sand in the buckets and on the canvas.

Graham picked up the knife from the still warm water, and shook it free of droplets.

'Grit your teeth man, you're in the Navy.' And he began to part the areas of tattered skin and flesh so that he could reach the shattered bone.

Mary felt sick. She felt the bile in her stomach heave up.

'Vomit over your shoulder, for God's sake,' snapped Graham. The injured man reached up and pressed her hand.

'If anything … happens … get word to my mother, tell her, please.'

Mary took hold of his good hand and pressed it.

'I promise.'

'Open!' Graham forced open the man's mouth, and pushed the leather gag between his teeth. Then he went back to work. The big knife pressed down into the wound, the bones flaked off as the surgeon sawed carefully. The groans were muted by the leather strap. Mary could see his teeth biting hard into it.

'Oh, oh oh!' The man choked in agony.

Mary felt the spew rising up again. She felt compelled to watch, she couldn't turn her eyes away. Forcing the bile back down into her stomach, she pressed hard down on the man's left shoulder, keeping it firm, and gripped his right hand tightly. She was thankful she was strong enough to keep up a powerful pressure. Graham cut down into the flesh just above the inner elbow, readying it for the teeth of the saw. He mopped the blood as it seeped out. Screams gurgled deep in the man's throat and he gripped Mary's hand so tightly that his nails pierced her own hand.

Graham picked up the saw and poised it above the cracked and broken bone.

The saw bit into the bone. The noise was that of butchering an animal, thought Mary. Only this, this was a live man. The smell of blood, of sand soaked in blood, made her feel dizzy. She tried to keep steady, but watching Graham pull back the flesh from the bone sickened her. She felt the bile wrenching and rising through her gut to her mouth. Only the grip of the man's hand kept her upright and helped her force the bile down again.

Bits of broken bone flaked off, and then – the saw was through the flesh and skin at the back of the arm. The man screamed.

'Enough! Oh God, make an end to this. Please.' The words were muffled but still the sound was piercing.

Thud! The arm dropped to the deck.

'Release your hold.' Graham commanded. She did so, and watched in surprise as the flesh slowly crept back over the end of the bone. Graham gave a release turn on the tourniquet and the arteries began to bleed a little.

'Why?' Mary forgot herself in asking.

'To allow me to see where to secure the major blood vessels.' Graham was threading a sealing fibre round a big blood vessel and the bleeding slowed to a trickle. She mopped it with a clean cloth. Graham continued his tying and the bleeding slowed, then stopped altogether.

'Cloths! Quickly!' the surgeon commanded. One of the boys handed him two of the pile of cloths they had ready. Graham stuffed these into the open wound, dusting it first with basilicum powder.

There was a mixture of spirits of turpentine on the table beside the surgeon: he dipped a cloth in it and applied it to the wound. The man screamed.

The boy passed over the cloths swiftly, helping Graham to stanch the blood. And then, the deed was done. The young man was moaning softly now. His forehead was wet with sweat, the stink of the wound and the blood was everywhere, and by the stench, Mary thought, he must have soiled himself.

Then the wound was bandaged, the man helped upright.

'A dose of laudanum later,' Graham said to the man. 'I'll give it you in the officers' mess.' Then to Mary and the boys, 'Clean up now!'

She groaned. The operation had taken all her strength, emotional, and physical. She wanted to breathe the fresh air, to take a draught of cool, fresh water, and to wash the perspiration off her hands and face. Her shirt and trousers were soaked with blood and sweat. Her neckcloth was awry.

She bent down. The sight of the severed arm made her so dizzy that she had to clutch the side of the chair. She vomited, all the repressed bile coming to the fore.

Graham looked down and smiled.

'That's the first one. The next will be better.' He called over one of the loblolly boys. 'Help here, clean up!'

Mary looked up gratefully. The boy was as white faced as she was, but together they swept the arm and the bone flakes into a sack, they cleaned the vomit with sand, and they wiped down the chair and took the sheet to be cleaned.

'Good,' Graham approved. 'Good! Take

some deep breaths and then back to work. Quick!'

She stumbled over to the rail. Her mind was full of the surgery, the man's pain, the skill and tension of the amputation. She felt she had been catapulted into a different world, where she was dangerously ignorant, unpractised and inexpert.

'Come on, now, Watson. Back to work. Hurry up!' She failed to recognise the speaker, but she certainly understood the words. Back to work.

CHAPTER TWENTY-TWO

It was evening. The day had passed in a blur of action. The ship was moving fast and smoothly. Mary stumbled back to the ship's rail and lifted her face to the winds. She needed time to think. It had been a long day assisting the surgeon. All that had happened in the last weeks was tumbling round in her mind. London, and Jem and Ewan Cameron. The conspirators. The prostitutes. Betty and her friend, Bobby. Cutting her hair, tying it back. On board. Harry. Then finding Jock beside him. The two friends, from Fife, from home.

More memories. The surgeon's orlop deck, the amputation. The amputation! Mary groaned as she remembered pressing hard down on the man's shoulder to keep him still as the surgeon's knife cut down through the flesh, sawed through the bone. She thought she would never forget the noise of the saw. But … she'd done what was wanted. She'd forgotten her own anguish in caring for the man both during and after the operation. She'd obeyed orders and she'd wanted to look after the man, to clean the wound, to pack it, to bathe his head. She wanted – yes, she did – she wanted to nurse. She wanted to learn more about this caring.

Her face and neck cooler now, her clothes dewed with spray, she turned back to the doorway. The deck was unusually quiet – the time of day meant that many seamen were eating, or below decks trying to snatch some sleep before going on watch.

A footstep made her start.

'Mary! Lass!'

'Oh, Harry! Harry!' She would have swung into his arms, but he stepped back and raised a warning finger.

'Remember! We have to be careful.'

She turned to face the sea.

'Aye. You're right. But … it's hard. And, and … I helped with an amputation.' She gulped on the word. It had just occurred to her that one day it might be Harry getting a ball in him.

'Oh! Aye, that'll have been tough. But give me more of your story.'

She took a deep breath.

'There's a man I met in the coach, called Ewan Cameron, and he was friendly with a London innkeeper called Jem, and they were both friendly with Mr Stott, the innkeeper in Leith. And he's the one that was askin' me to look out for his son, Archie. I'll have to tell Mr Cameron I've found him.'

Harry shook his head in bewilderment.

'Slow down!' he begged. 'I've heard about Setton's family and the Auld Alliance. What he's doin' here we can only guess. Jock thinks, and I agree with him, that he's got some mates here, some special pals …'

'That's likely! The short of it is, I think Mr Cameron and Jem are men we can trust. See here, when you went off with the press gang …' And Mary recounted again the story of clutching Setton's coat, and the piece of paper sliding out. She passed over leaving home, but said that Jock's Jeannie had been very upset, though fine with the bairn growing in her. And she went on quickly to say she thought Setton had followed her to London, just for that fragment of paper. When she described her meeting with Mr Cameron and Jem, and the fitting together of a document, Harry stopped her.

'Are you sure you're no' making this up?' he asked. In spite of the seriousness of the occasion, she had to smile.

'No, I'm not, it's all real, Harry. We're in something big.'

She finished the tale with Setton's menaces to her and Mr Cameron's low-voiced explanations. Harry scratched his red head.

'Last month, Mary my lass, we were in Fife, rattling around, havin' a good time. And now …'

'And now, we're in a … terrifying position,' she finished for him.

'That's for sure!' he groaned. 'We need to keep Jock in the picture. He's been thinkin', like you say, that Setton's a baddie, and we need to be careful. He's taken his measure, that's for sure.''

Jock was a shrewd man, Mary knew. She nodded.

'Best introduce him to Mr Cameron then. Mr Cameron said just to keep watch on our friend. And maybe, we need to watch ourselves too, to make sure we don't slip up.'

He nodded.

'I'm off to turn in. I'm on watch later. I'll keep my eyes skinned, that's sure.'

And with a touch on her shoulder, he turned and walked along the deck to the steps leading to their mess.

She continued staring at the sea. She expected to be working again that night for Graham so a bit more fresh air, she thought, one more deep breath, then I'm off to tidy up for the night. As she pushed her hair back, a hand touched her shoulder and slid down her arm, grasping her elbow. She turned, startled.

'Ah Mistress, do not start so, I did not mean to startle you.' The voice purred behind her.

She closed her eyes. Setton! Not again, not now! Please!

'I will not go away, Mistress. Open your eyes. We have things to discuss.'

'We have nothing to discuss, sir, I am here on my own business. Pray excuse me.'

'Stay!' His voice was compelling, as was his grasp on her arm.

She was obliged to stand still. For a seaman to twist away from an officer was to invite reproof, and worse still, punishment.

'Well, sir?'

'I do not know your game, Mistress, but I have my own will to oversee here. I beg you will not get in my way. Or else …'

She was tempted to demand what 'or else' meant. But she had not yet discussed with Harry how either of them was to respond to Setton, should he challenge them. Challenge! Maybe that was the word to keep in mind.

'Or else, sir?'

'I may enlighten the Captain as to some of his crew. That one of them has a document … mayhap dishonest, mayhap to speak of treason?'

'*We* are no traitors, sir, we are loyal to our country.'

'And who would believe an idler and a pressed man?'

'Against a Lieutenant, sir?'

'Correct.'

'A challenge, sir. I am to … keep out of your way. And perhaps, to be discreet. And in turn, you, sir, will be discreet also?'

'You will not find me ungrateful, Mistress. To you or to your husband.'

The hand was withdrawn. He turned and moved off, his footsteps soft on the deck. She let out a deep sigh, breathing out a prayer.

'Dear God, help us, please help us.' And added, in her head, because it seemed too selfish to utter. 'Please, please, let us get back home, back to Scotland, keep it safe, our country.' The thought of the Fife coast, the tumbling seas, the fish hurtling in on the tide, the journeys to St Andrews through the barley fields with the poppies bright … she blinked the tears from her eyes. Back to work! she snapped out her internal commands.

In the quarters before the orlop deck, the sick bay, she found a couple of loblolly boys tending to someone wrapped in blankets.

'A new sick man,' one of them said, 'with a fever. Surgeon said he was to be moved here from his mess in case of infection.' He got up to go, his duty done for the evening.

The sick man was tossing and turning, and groaning. He was muttering. She bent down to listen. This wasn't English. Surely, surely he was speaking French. She turned her head to look for Graham, but he was absent. Only the other loblolly boy was in sight, folding away clean blankets.

Mary wrung out a cloth in warm water. She bent over the sick man and touched his shoulder to warn him of treatment to come.

'I'm Watson,' she said in English, 'Harry Watson.' He opened his eyes and stared at her, fuzzily.

'Pierre … non, Peter … Pierre Lavalle … Peter Lovell …'

Her eyes widened. French? Then English. What could this mean? Should she tell the surgeon?

She began to wipe the man's forehead, hoping that more words would come out, but he seemed to be sinking back into unconsciousness.

'Oh, wake up, come on, wake up,' she muttered through gritted teeth. Strange, she thought, how she was still sympathetic to him now, with his obvious pain and distress, even though she knew he was a Frenchman. Had he enlisted with the British navy? Or was he that dreadful thing, a spy? One of Setton's allies?

She looked round cautiously. Would it be noticed if she went into his pockets? After all, she could have promised to write to his wife. So, was she justified in searching his pockets? Her hand crept under the sheet, and slid down further to his trousers. Left hand pocket produced nothing, but in the right hand pocket, there was something. A fragment of paper, a small fragment which might have fitted into the pieces held now by Mr Cameron. She slid it quickly into her own trouser pocket to look at later.

'Watson!' the roar behind her made her start. Had Graham seen anything?

'Aye, aye sir?'

'We will soon have more custom. We'll need more sand brought down here.'

She hurried up to the deck, and struggled back down with two sandbags.

'That's no job for a woman, is it?' Graham

said softly, taking one from her.

'Sir!' she managed, horrified.

He turned back.

'There are many women on board. If you wish to resume your womanhood, you may still work with me. But in the meantime, I will continue to call you Watson. Have no fear.'

'My husband was pressed. I wanted to be with him. I thought … this might be the best way.'

The surgeon bowed his head.

'You make a fine loblolly boy, Watson.'

She carried on with the work, her mind stirring with questions and anxieties. Graham made no mention of her secret again: indeed, he treated her just like the boys, barking out his orders, making his demands clear.

But Mary could hardly wait to tell Harry their secret had been discovered. And if Mr Graham knew, and Setton, and Mr Cameron, how many others would guess? She could scarcely hold back rushing up to their favourite meeting place to tell him. Free from duties in the early hours of the morning, she scrambled on to the deck to find him.

'Mary!' he burst out.

'Harry!' she whispered in the same

moment.

'You first,' Harry said.

'Mr Graham, the surgeon, knows I'm a woman, but he won't say anything.'

'Right!' It seemed less important to him than his own news. 'Jock saw signals from a French ship when we were on watch during the night.'

'Signals?'

'Aye, lights flashing on and off. Not from a deck, or lookout, but from beside a gun. Jock counted which gun port it was, he thinks, but he could be mistaken. And he took a note of the number of shorts and longs but can make nothing of it. We have to speak to Mr Cameron.'

She nodded agreement.

'Let's go and find him now, if we can. And look at this! I was looking after a sick man, and found … this!' She produced the fragment of paper. Harry looked at it, turned it round, and peered again.

'Looks to me like a bit of French, but I was never good at reading and writing.' He fingered it again and it crunched under his touch. She grabbed it.

'Careful!' she warned. 'I've got to get it to Mr Cameron fast as I can.'

CHAPTER TWENTY-THREE

How would they find Mr Cameron quickly, she wondered? Harry and Jock had met him face to face earlier, so they might know where Cameron was to be found.

'I'm going to try on that deck. Maybe you should come too. Can you?'

'And miss the Mess food?' They grinned at each other. 'We've got some extras tucked away,' said Harry. 'Let's miss the food.'

'We'll be missed. Or, rather, you'll be missed,' Mary told him. 'I'd better just go myself and find Mr Cameron.'

'Not likely. Both.'

They walked off briskly to the upper gun deck. She walked warily along the deck, moving carefully between the groups of seamen huddled round the guns, avoiding the gun captains and the powder monkeys checking the guns, and fetching the powder.

'Jock! Jock!' They saw a friendly face.

'Aye?'

'We're looking for Mr Cameron.'

'Up yonder.' Jock pointed towards the bow, and was immediately shouted at. 'Pay attention! Get over here.'

He grinned at Mary and ran off.

Mr Cameron was where Jock had indicated, peering at an instrument in his hand, calculating, she thought, wind, weather, distance to the French fleet, their sails clear in the distance.

He spotted them.

'News?' He would know it must be important, to bring them up on deck before their scheduled meetings.

'Aye, sir.' She touched her forelock, determined to observe the formalities in case she herself was observed.

'Another piece of paper, sir, and here 'tis.' She produced it from her pocket. 'Came from a man who called himself Pierre Lavalle, then switched to Peter Lovell.'

He stared at her.

'Lavalle? Pierre Lavalle? Here on this ship? That's one of the big names in the network! We've got them!'

'And Harry says Jock saw signals from a gunport in the early hours of the morning.'

Harry nodded.

Mr Cameron stared at her.

'Signals from a gunport! Which ship? What were they?'

Harry produced the note outlining Jock's rendition of the code: short short short …

'And which gunport – roughly speaking?'

'Maybe you'd be best to come and see Jock, sir,' said Harry. 'He can tell you more exactly, mayhap, which ship it was.'

Harry led the way back to where Jock was standing in his gun crew. He beckoned. 'Jock, Mr Cameron wants a word.'

Jock saluted, and at a word from Harry he began to explain, pointing out a French ship a little apart from the enemy fleet.

'I can tell you which gunport, sir?' And he counted along ten gunports on the ship, facing the British fleet, until he came to the centre. 'That's the one, sir, I'd swear to it. Or near enough.'

Cameron stared at it.

'Not an official signal, then … Did you see anyone respond here?' Jock shook his head, disappointed. 'From the angle, it looks as if this was the ship they were aiming at, doesn't it? And with Pierre Lavalle on board, no doubt they were trying to reach him – or one of his allies.'

The name again reminded Mary of her other duties.

'Sir, I'll have to go.'

'One minute … Watsons and Jock.' Mr Cameron was grinning broadly. He touched the side of his hat. 'Well done!'

Jock saluted, Harry touched his forelock, and ran back down to the hammocks. Mary smiled in reply, the smile that lit up her face and eyes, and, so Cameron thought, brightened the day. He sighed.

Mary ran down to the surgeon's quarters, relieved. There were a few things she wanted to complete before seeking rest. The note and the signals were in good hands, she felt. The sickbay was dark, candlelit and stuffy. She moved around it carefully.

When Graham, the surgeon, came in, he found her looking over the stores in drawers, cupboards and particularly in the surgeon's chests.

'Busy, Watson?'

'Aye, sir, just thought I'd finish up tidying the bandages and such-like.'

'Carry on.' He left her to her work.

'Aye aye sir.'

She made sure she knew where all the instruments were, in case she needed to pass Mr Graham something quickly during the battle to come. The bandages she rolled up tighter. She checked that the powders were in good order. There were too few bandages she thought, so she bent to open a cupboard door, to see if there were any more bandages stored. A noise made her stiffen and move out of sight of the half open sickbay door into the big cupboard, almost closing herself in. A chink of light came through the opening.

'Chut, chut!' The noise came again. A cautious whisper, the sound of secrets about to be shared.

'What is't?'

'Shh. We must make a move soon.'

'How? The captain is surrounded by his men all day, we can't get near the wheel. And Lavalle here is too ill.'

'Aye, we can do it. There have been signals. And I've been talking with the Lieutenant. We can take over if we take the guns with us, we can master the wheel, the man steering, the man taking soundings. With them doing our will, we can sail the ship over to the French.'

'Hush … there might be someone around, maybe in the orlop.'

The padding sound of footsteps moving away released Mary from her hideout. At least, she thought, she was free to go about her business. She straightened up, rubbing her back, some bandages in her hand. Rats scurried along the sides of the deck but she ignored them.

The door slammed back to the deck pillar. She looked up in alarm.

'What are you doing in here?' The voice was the same as the one she'd heard whispering on the deck.

'Pardon, sir, I am but checking and tidying the table for Mr Graham. And also checking the powders and the materials he may need. I am learning to be a surgeon's assistant, I do hope.'

The man's eyes narrowed, his lips sneered. 'A surgeon's assistant, forsooth … best you get cut there and fight!'

'I do what I am bid. And I am bid be a help to the surgeon here.'

Suddenly Graham himself loomed in the doorway.

'Mackintosh? Be about your business.'

The man moved reluctantly out of the doorway, and Graham turned to Mary.

'Be about your business too! We have no time for idle bodies here.'

'Aye aye sir!' Mary rolled the bandages tighter, and put them back on the shelf, shutting the door firmly. 'I was making sure I knew where everything was, sir, for the battle.'

'If you go on like this, I might see that you are rated as permanent surgeon's assistant.' He nodded and went out, moving easily to the sway of the ship.

She took a last look at the sleeping patients and blew out the candles. Back on the crowded gun deck, she found herself amongst the swaying hammocks of those on four-hour watch. One of these was Harry. She stood at the foot of his hammock, watching with love his deep sleep. Or was it? As she began to move away, one eye opened. His face split in a huge grin as he saw her. He moved easily in the swaying hammock and slid on to the deck in a matter of seconds, far more easily and gracefully than she did when she clambered in and out. His shoes were already on his feet, and he shrugged on his jacket as he tiptoed to join her. He touched her shoulder as their eyes met. Mary sighed. How long would this go on for? He hitched up his hammock.

'What news?' he breathed in her ear as, like two seamen side by side, they moved purposefully on to the upper deck.

'Cameron will be on deck during your watch. And I overheard Mackintosh talking about guns and sailing the ship to the French.' She kept her voice low.

'All right, I'll take it from here. You get some sleep.'

The tramp of feet on the deck broke their conversation. Harry went to take up his watch. And Mary slid back to her own hammock, lost in thought.

She'd got what she wanted, she told herself, to be near Harry. She didn't want him so far away and herself ignorant of what was going on. Now she wanted to keep safe and to protect them both as far as she was able. And she was sure that Harry wanted to protect her too, and get them both back safely on shore, and thence to Scotland.

But with a battle expected as well as the conditions on board ship, how were they to manage?

CHAPTER TWENTY-FOUR

October 20th, and it was a chilly evening again. A wind ruffled the water into short choppy waves. Mary stumbled to the deck rail and lifted her face to the winds, hungering for fresh cool air after a day helping the surgeon. It had been hard enough work. Tidying, cleaning, anointing. Sickness, and a few injuries such as broken limbs from slipping on deck – she held the bandages and supports for the surgeon and reassured the patients as best she could. Bloody fists and a broken shoulder – from what she could only guess as a fight on board. No one enlightened her. The treatments for now still took place on deck, where the light was better. Even as they were tucked away in a corner, the noise of the seamen on deck and the distant firing of guns resounded in her ears. But the fresh air was healing.

She let out a deep sigh, breathing out a prayer. Home! Scotland, and safety. She could think of nothing else, on this broad sea, this big ship, this terrifying situation, men wounded, men killed – but she withdrew to home in her mind.

There was a shout from the fo'c'sle. Could it be Lieutenant Setton, after her again?

She turned and ran quickly down to the orlop deck, looking neither to right nor left, making sure she was out of the way of any hostile intent.

In the sickbay she found the Frenchman, if that was what he was, Pierre Lavalle, moaning and groaning in his fever. A loblolly boy was swabbing his head with cool water, but handed the job over to her. She moved to the head of the bunk and began to soothe him.

A noise, footsteps maybe. She stiffened and leaned forward to tuck in the blanket.

'Ah, Mistress, well done.' Again, she heard that soft purring voice with menace in its tones. He was crowding her into the side of the deck, always looming over her with his powerful shoulders and muscled thighs. She smelt the acrid smell of gunpowder and shuddered. It was Setton again! He must have followed her down. Was she never to be free of this man?

'I have discovered a calling, sir, I aim to make a nurse.'

'And a fine one, too.'

'Are you not needed on deck, sir? I make no mistake, your seamanship must be wanted by the Captain, is that not so?' She kept her voice low so that nothing would disturb the sick man. She turned to her charge, putting a wet cloth to his mouth and damping the dry lips. The boys had gone, and Setton moved closer. She hoped no one was watching.

'If you please, mistress,' Lieutenant Setton's hand brushed against her neck and shoulder. Its message was unmistakable. This man would have her if he could, if she would allow herself to be attracted. She stared up into his smiling face. His shadowy eyes sent an invitation. He bent his head. She forced herself not to shudder, to turn her blushing cheek away, looking down in feigned embarrassment. Better that he should think her an easy woman, than that he should speak against her and Harry and get them into trouble. A quick glance round the orlop deck showed it to be empty nearby with loblolly boys clustered round the companionway. No one was watching them.

'No, sir … no …' She looked down again, and then coquettishly, at Setton from under her eyelashes. He relaxed, smiling, clearly certain of his conquest.

'I shall be in touch, mistress. You understand?' He laid his hand on her arm, and she could only hope that the tension in her wrist he would attribute to attraction, rather than hatred.

He moved away. She forced herself to continue her care of the sick man, though all she wanted was to find Harry. She shuddered at the memory of Setton's touch. Harry would be furious, she knew, but … was it better for them both for her to play along with Setton's desires, at least to a point? She needed to talk to Harry.

She wrung out her cloths, spread them on a nearby bench, and decided to grab some time off before moving to another patient.

'I won't be long,' she muttered to the nearest loblolly boy.

Up the stairs again. She counted this was her sixth time up and down these stairs since she began work this morning.

Harry wasn't on watch. He wasn't in his hammock either. Where could he be? She was desperate to see him, to touch him, to push away the sickening memory of Setton's advances.

She spotted Jock and gestured to him, mouthing,

'Harry?'

He shook his head, and there was no Harry to be seen. But Jock stayed within earshot. Clearly, he had been detailed to keep an eye on her and manage her safety. She wished it was Harry. Disconsolately, she returned to the sick quarters.

When Graham, the surgeon, came in, he found her looking at the patients, checking their bandages, feeling their foreheads.

'Busy, Watson?'

'Aye, sir, just thought I'd check the men here.'

'Are we ready for the battle?'

'Aye aye, sir.'

'Well done. Good. Carry on.'

The battle! Mary thought. The battle! Nothing but the battle. For a moment she tried to imagine – men would be killed, injured in a horrendous and terrifying rain of shot. And all she could do was bind up the wounds. She blinked tears away before they spilled over.

'Aye aye sir.'

He moved away, and she was left by herself. There were a few patients lying down in the sick bay. They had been treated and were being watched for now: soon the least serious would be cleared to make way for others. She took a quick look round. No need for her at the moment, so she was by herself, with no precise instructions and tasks to hand.

It was good to be quiet in this crowded ship. Even with the rats scurrying around and squealing, it was still a quieter space. The noise of running men on the decks above rumbled in her ears, but there were no cannons – as yet.

But it was not good to be able to think, reflect, to plan, have ideas and to grieve for the miseries about to happen. She walked to the ladder and climbed again to the top. Men were moving purposefully over the rigging, powder monkeys running to the guns, the noise was of feet running, moving, bosun and others shouting, giving orders. Restless, she turned back down to the silent sick quarters, and nervously went again to look at the table where the surgeon would lay out his instruments. Was she ready?

She heard a creaking noise, as of a door moving, and looked round. There was no one to be seen, but one door was half open, and she thought that she had shut all the doors. There was a shadow, cast by the light sneaking down the steps. She crouched down behind the table.

'Hush! Hush!' A cautious whisper sounded outside the door. 'We can talk inside here. Surgeon's up with Captain.'

'The boys? The patients?'

'In the sickbay. Come on …'

Two men strode through the half open door.

'It comes time to make a move.'

Another man joined in.

'Is anyone in the sickbay?' The familiar voice came from the end of the orlop deck. Mary froze in her place. Pray God he hadn't seen her.

'Good sirs, the sickbay is quiet right now. Patients are resting. If we keep our voices low …'

The first man spoke.

'How can we make a move? We are but few.'

A taller shadow slid through the door.

'Aye, we can.'

The last man shut the door.

'I have our guns here, primed and loaded. The plan I have is this,' and he lowered his voice even further. She listened harder. 'I will rush the Captain and his closest lieutenant. You, sir, will take out the man at the wheel. And you both will cover the quarterdeck. There will be help there too.'

Mary was aghast. The low voice continued.

'Then we will command the ship.'

'Aye, but there's not many of us.' The voice was surly.

'There are many, many, more than you realise. And we have the advantage of surprise. Now is our chance, on the eve of the battle. We'll take the ship over to the French.'

'An uprising!' muttered one voice.

'And well paid for it!' replied Setton. 'Money! More than you've ever seen.' If he had motive beyond that, he kept it to himself.

Paid by the French, to betray his country. She was disgusted. There was nowhere for her to run, no one to call out to. She was scared that the men would move nearer her hiding place. Her eyes searched the area for another hiding space. Ah, she had it! Just behind the dispensing table was a curtained-off area. She crept on all-fours silently towards it. But the roll of the ship, unexpectedly strong, slid her further than she wanted to go, and she slithered into a chair too quickly to stop herself.

Perhaps she'd made some sort of noise. Perhaps there was the sound of a slithering motion. She had certainly disturbed a nest of rats and several of them ran out. A real betrayal. She backed away as she heard footsteps nearing the table. She was spotted!

'There IS someone here. Come!'

The other men surrounded her. She was trapped. Her hands flew to her mouth, a scream forming. The larger of the two men slammed his hand over her mouth, the other grabbed her wrists and dragged her up.

She tried to pull away, wrestling with her captors, stumbling towards the doorway.

'You're coming with us.'

'He's listening to us. He's heard us.'

Setton beckoned.

'Take … him away. He knows too much.'

'What'll we do with him?'

'How about over the side?' Setton grinned evilly at her. 'Or … he comes over to our side. With me.' He leered at her again, closer this time, bending over her.

Mary screamed. One of the sailors slapped his hand over her mouth again.

'But search him first! He's got something I want. A bit of paper.' Setton was keeping up the pretence of her disguise.

Her head in a lock under the left arm of one sailor and her own arms nearly wrenched out of her sockets, her feet trapped between the boots of one of the men, she felt them scrounging in her pockets.

'Nothing there, sir!'

Oh, why didn't someone come? Where was everyone? One or two of the patients must have heard, but were unable to move to help. What about the other boys?

She tried to bite the nearest hand and the man twisted his other hand round her hair braid and pulled her head to the side.

She squirmed her face clear of the restraining hand and yelled,

'Help!' Furiously, she sank her teeth into the palm. He roared.

'What's all this?' Surgeon Graham loomed in the doorway.

'A bad man here, Surgeon Graham, we do but ensure some discipline,' Setton snapped out.

Graham glanced at Mary.

'Bad? This one? What's the charge?'

'Obstructing an officer in his business.'

'Rubbish!' Graham snapped. 'I've never had a better assistant.' He turned to the men.

'Mackintosh? Jones? Be about your business. And as for you, sir ...' He was about to berate Setton, but the man had gone. He turned to Mary.

'What's all that about?'

'An uprising! They're planning an uprising!' She began to explain, but he held up his hand. 'Lieutenant Setton? A mutineer? That is hard to believe. This attack will take time to sort out. The captain may not believe a loblolly boy. You may be the one in irons! No time at the moment. You can tell me more later.'

He didn't believe her, she was sure. That was a put-off.

She was rubbing her shoulders and arms, still shaking from her ordeal. He gave her a sympathetic look.

'Just get about your business and we'll keep this secret until I have time to tell the captain.' Better, but still a put-off, she thought. Did that mean anything? Was Graham one of them?

She had found some liniment and rubbed her arms with it, and her neck where the seaman had tried to twist her head.

'Aye aye, sir.' She was hoarse from screaming, tearful, and still numb with the alarm of what had happened to her. He eyed her keenly as she tried to pull herself together, rubbing her shoulders, rubbing her sore face and throat.

'Go get some fresh air.'

She stumbled from his searching gaze,

moving up to the gun deck amongst the swaying hammocks, desperate to find Harry, or even Lieutenant Cameron, to share the burden of this awful knowledge.

Luckily, she spotted Harry this time on the first gun deck.

'What happened to you?' he asked. 'Let's find a quiet corner.'

Up to the deck, aided by a shove on her hips from his powerful hands.

'Right. Now we can speak.'

'But carefully now,' she warned. He led her to an isolated part of the deck. 'Setton's men grabbed me. I'm sore from his handling.'

'What?'

'But … Harry,' her voice was gleeful, despite still feeling shaky from the attack. 'I bit one of them.'

'Hahahahah –' He stopped abruptly as she put her hand over his mouth.

'Sssssh.'

'What have you learned?'

She recited all she'd learned from Setton and his on-coming ways, to the whispered colloquy outside the orlop deck door and to the attack, when he'd suggested she be thrown overboard.

'You're in real danger. You know too much!' he said anxiously.

'But what can we do?' she asked.

Harry leaned on the deckrail while she stood with her back to it, keeping an eye out for anyone passing. The first man she saw was Mr Cameron.

'I'll try to keep near you,' said Harry.

'And I also, Mistress.' Ewan Cameron must have been in time to hear her story. 'This is serious. Thanks to you both, Harry Watson, and to your friend Jock, we have uncovered two ships with potential rebels.'

'Surgeon Graham says there's no time to warn the captain.' Mary began. 'And that he wouldn't listen to me.'

'Is *he* safe?' asked Harry. Cameron nodded.

'Quite safe, I believe, and totally focussed on his job. And I shall tell him immediately – and also warn him of your danger. We must find a way to protect you.'

They all looked at each other, sick with anger.

'Confusion to Boney!' Harry said. Cameron nodded again.

'Indeed. We must work towards that.'

They moved apart, Harry to go back to his hammock, to rest after his watch, Cameron, to go she knew not where, and herself back to the surgeon's quarters.

Back in the orlop deck, she moved round the surgeon's table. The candles wanted replacing: they were guttering in their holders. She snuffed them, and eased them out of the holders. Before she put new ones in, she thought she'd better scour out the holders properly, so that new candles would sit firmly and give a good light.

A strong knife, that's what's wanted, she mused, and pulled open drawer after drawer in search of an ordinary strong knife, not one of the surgeon's special knives. When she found her tool, she carried it over to what she called the 'candle table', the stand which the surgeon used to hold the candles so he could see to operate. There she laid out the holders, and began to scour them, one by one, shaking them free of wax, wiping them, and placing new candles in them, ready to be lit and fixed. And all the time her thoughts were with Setton and Cameron, and the paper. She hoped she could trust Mr Cameron. But truth to tell, she felt she could trust only Harry – and perhaps Graham, the surgeon. She had never been so fearful before in her life.

CHAPTER TWENTY-FIVE

Before her night watch with the sick men, Mary went on deck. The sky was clear and the stars were out. The moon was a beautiful circle. Mary gazed in wonder: that moon, these stars were looking down on the shores of Fife too, on Leith and on London, and all her friends. They were all part of the same world. But the skies also covered France and the wicked Bonaparte and his revolutionaries. She blinked back some tears. Home was very dear to her, but, she had to admit, there were parts of this adventure that she had come to love. Being with Harry, of course, and also working with the sick and injured. Mistress Wood had been right, she thought, she did love caring for people.

'Mistress!' She turned, aghast. It was Setton. He held up a hand. 'I'm not here to harass you, Mistress, but see if we can do a deal.'

Mary thought she saw a shadow to her right. Cameron had said that someone would be detailed to watch her wherever she went. Maybe the shadow was the watcher. If so, she hoped he would come forward.

She slid one foot behind the other and slipped backwards until she had almost reached the stairs to the lower deck.

'Ahhhh!' Setton lunged forward and grabbed her wrist, pulling her towards him. His strength was infinitely greater than hers, and the fury in his face terrified her. She struggled against his grasp. 'Give it to me.'

'Let her go!' The shadow materialised into Harry, and he was beside them in an instant.

'Indeed?' Setton held her still, and he had a pistol in his hand. 'So you're the husband? Then you won't want to see your wife hurt, will you?' His purring tones could just be heard above her cry as he grabbed her shoulder, spun her round with her back to him, and jabbed the pistol in her ribs. 'Stand still!' His arm went round her shoulders, pinning her arms to her sides.

'Stand still?' echoed Harry, eyes narrowed. 'What do you want with us, Mister?'

'Sir, or I'll have you flogged!'

'I don't say Sir to a traitor!' snapped Harry louder than he'd spoken before.

'Silence!' ordered Setton, giving an extra thrust to the pistol in Mary's ribs. She squealed with pain. She tried to turn her head. Harry was working something out, she knew, and there was Jock, too, creeping up from the side, trying to get near Harry and to attract Setton's attention.

A look from Harry. They knew each other so well, she knew what that look meant. And despite her fear, or maybe because of it, she intended to act on it. She had the Scots 'wha daur meddle with me' attitude in her head, and her anger at the traitors overcame her fears. Besides, she was now with friends – Harry and Jock together.

She closed one eye in a droopy half wink, which, from their childhood days, meant 'look out!' And in an instant, while Jock yelled, and Harry took a nimble step forward, hands outstretched to pull her away, she'd wrenched herself sideways and down, while at the same time her hand managed to jerk Setton's pistol hand upwards and to the side. It was a risky move. The shot could have entered her side. But Setton's attention had been diverted. And she'd been sufficiently quick. The three Fifers had acted together, and she was free!

The resulting pistol crack brought men running to the stairway.

Someone seized Setton, still with gun in hand.

'Lieutenant, what's going on here? Gun practice is in the stern.'

He broke free.

'COME, MEN! Our chance is now!'

His shout hurtled across the decks and several men came running, weaving in and out of the crowd on deck and with pistols at the ready.

'One of you, get the others!' Setton yelled. 'The rest of you, FOLLOW ME!'

And he turned and ran through the gathering crowd to the quarterdeck and towards the Captain's cabin, brandishing his gun as he went. He was followed by half a dozen men, cutlasses at the ready.

'He's going for the Captain,' Jock yelled. 'After him!'

Others were shouting.

'We'll take over the ship!'

'Then we join the Frenchies.'

'Over my dead body,' someone else shouted.

'Out cutlasses!' yelled someone else.

The men with cutlasses flourished them,

whirled them in the air and plunged forward, yelling and shouting. Others waded into the fight, fists raised, kicking out at the mutineers.

'Rebels! Rebels!' yelled someone on the quarterdeck.

Harry grabbed Mary's sleeve.

'Come on, come on!'

She ran beside him. They dodged in and out of the milling sailors. Shots were fired: the yells and cracks were horrendous. Mary recognised several of her messmates and others she'd befriended, fighting each other.

'Move!' Harry hauled her up the stairs to the quarterdeck. At the top he let go her sleeve. He was heading towards the wheel. Jock followed him. Mary ran beside them and saw Setton standing at the wheel, his pistol in the ribs of the helmsman though he could not have had time to reload.

'Steer for starboard,' he roared.

'I takes my orders from the captain!' the man bellowed. Setton grabbed the wheel with his free hand and tried to turn it. Harry dived into action, seized Setton by his legs and yanked. The man fell sideways, the pistol spinning across the deck. Harry sat on his legs, while Jock seized the pistol. He aimed it at Setton, squirming on the ground.

'Dinna fire, dinna fire!' screamed Mary. There had been too much violence already. 'Harry! Watch out!'

Ignoring Mary's anguish, Jock pulled the trigger, but nothing happened. Instead Setton took advantage of Jock's surprise to wriggle free. Harry tried to snatch him again but missed as Setton tore up the stairs to the Captain.

'Surrender!' he yelled, drawing a second pistol. 'Surrender! And take the ship to starboard.'

Captain Masterman lunged but this pistol fired. The captain fell forward, a ribbon of blood trickling from his shoulder.

'Aux armes!' yelled Setton.

Mary shuddered into the corner of a doorway, and stared in horror at the scene on the upper gundeck. The fighting had spread, she could see, with more and more men joining in. Someone was holding the ship steady, but she could see two mutineers beside the helmsman, pistols pointing at his head.

She clung to the doorway, numb with shock and fear. Where was Harry, oh where *was* he? She risked a glance around the quarterdeck. He was nowhere to be seen. Her eyes roved across the fighters on the lower deck. Was he there? No, she thought not. A slight movement to her left made her turn her head. She managed to suppress a scream. Harry was climbing up a rope to the poop deck. Clearly, he meant to sneak up behind Setton and capture him. Someone else had the same idea. She recognised Ewan Cameron, inching along carefully, holding a bit of wood as a shield, and his pistol at the ready. He spotted Harry, now on deck, and beckoned with his pistol hand. The hand indicated 'keep low' and Harry dropped to his knees and began to wriggle forward, almost hidden in the shadow of a big chest. Setton was standing forward on the poop deck yelling encouragement to the fighters, waving his pistol. She could see one or two bodies on the deck, and thin trickles of blood running, joining to make a river.

'Fight on! FIGHT ON! We're winning!' yelled Setton. 'Allons! Pour la France!' In his rush to encourage the mutineers, his gaze was fixed forward.

Cameron beckoned to Harry 'Come!' The two men rushed together and grabbed Setton. Cameron seized his pistol hand, while Harry twisted his other arm behind his back.

'It's over!' yelled Cameron. 'Mutineers! Surrender!'

Several of the men stopped suddenly and stared up at him. Jock picked up Setton's pistol from the deck and held it high above his head.

'Come on, men, loyal to Scotland, and to England!' A mutineer tried to grab at his sleeve, but was pulled back by a loyalist. Jock held firm to the pistol and pointed it at the group of mutineers, while the loyalists seized their chance and grabbed at as many mutineers as they could reach.

But Setton made a sudden twist, wrenching free from Ewan Cameron and jerking his arm upwards.

'Aux armes! To the French ships!'

But the French ships, Mary suddenly saw, were now perilously close. The Captain, clutching his shoulder, was issuing orders, paying little heed to the mutineers, leaving them to his crew to deal with.

Harry gripped more tightly, but Setton managed to pull free, ducked and kicked Harry in the groin in a sideways move. He tore off, leaving Harry sprawled on the deck. Cameron staggered. Setton leaped down the steps and grabbed Mary, dragging her along with him. He pushed his way through the countless seamen moving towards the decks. They took no notice of the captive sailor, as she seemed to them. Battle was close and they needed to prepare. She screamed and struggled, trying to slow down the villain, to let Harry and Jock and maybe Cameron catch them up.

'Stop him!' yelled Cameron. Harry pulled

himself back up, clutching his knee.

Setton reached a lower deck. He pushed Mary before him as a shield, ensuring his safety and the withdrawal of her supporters. And hearing Setton's yells, the deck was filling with mutineers, scenting victory. Most seamen were on the upper decks and were manning the guns, with little time to spare for yells and shouts of mutiny. But the mutineers had kept together. They seized the few loyalists on the deck and pushed them to the side of the ship.

'Join us! Or we push you over!'

Mary heard yells and splashes as she struggled with her captor.

Down further they went, Mary wriggling and dragging her heels as best she could, down past the deck swabbers, down to the lower gundeck. The rebels clattered after them. But this seemed a minor incident compared with battle preparation, so there were only casual glances at the noisy group.

She could hide among these gun crews, Mary thought. *If* she could only get free. Setton forced her along the deck despite her yells and squirming to get free. She managed to turn her head. She saw Harry's red hair. He was at the bottom of the stairs, pausing, searching for her, head turning this way and that. Beside him, Jock had a hand on his shoulder, his finger pointed towards Setton and herself.

'Harry!' she got her mouth clear from Setton's restraining hand. 'Here! Aaaargh!' The gurgle faded as Setton yanked her head back, his arm round her throat. Had she not been so valuable to him as a hostage, he would have killed her, she knew.

But Harry had heard. He came running towards her, ducking and diving, twisting and turning, finding his way through the gun crews, weaving towards her, dodging in and out of the guns. He came to the big gun where she was held. She could see his red hair above the barrel, but she was powerless to scream, or even to move a muscle, so tightly did Setton hold her.

Then the red head disappeared below the gun barrel. Setton twisted her head to the side again. No Harry! No rescue! She was weeping with pain, with fear and with desperate disappointment. Her throat hurt with his grip, her neck screamed in pain with being jerked and twisted. Her shoulders ached with pulling and being pulled. She closed her eyes. Setton drew her further amongst the big guns being run in and out of the hull, a final practice for the battle to come.

The grip on her shoulders and arms tightened even more. Her eyes flew open. She writhed in the tight grasp, trying to ease its unyielding pressure, and trying to catch a glimpse of where Harry or Jock might be.

Setton pulled her body back further against him, trapping her arms behind her. She could see better now and stared from her teary eyes as best she could, trying to distinguish Harry or Jock in the midst of the gun crews. But neither could be seen.

In fact, Harry was well hidden behind Jock. Jock had picked up a cutlass and was forging a passage through the noisy busy crowd. A bigger man than Harry, he shouldered his way between the gun crews, twisting this way and that, cutting a passage. Men moved out of his way, and Harry wriggled in his wake, dodging all obstacles.

At last, he was through the crowd! All the attention was on avoiding the sweeping cutlass, and no one had noticed the crouching, wriggling sailor squeezing through behind. As he slid behind one big gun, preparing for his rescue manoeuvre, Harry signalled over to Jock, a finger movement indicating Setton and palm down indicating hush. Jock jerked his thumb up, and moved forward slowly, trying to engage Setton's notice, and keep him from seeing Harry.

Setton, now with his own knife, was watching Jock moving carefully towards him. But he missed seeing Harry, who, with one rapid movement, leaped out at the traitor, turning him sharply. Setton's knife flew upwards as he staggered under the onslaught and yelled. Jock pulled him off balance from behind. Men came running. The nearest gun captain sprang into action, and seized Setton's arm.

'None of that on my gundeck.' Another gunner grabbed the knife. Setton panted,

'They're traitors. They're traitors. Get them.' The sailors slowly released him and he staggered upright. 'MEN! TO ME! TO ME!' More running feet, rebels running to Setton's aid, pushing aside any opposition from the gun crews.

But Mary was free. Fear overcame her aches and she backed away, towards Harry. Harry grabbed her arm, pulling her behind him. Like Jock, he had a cutlass in his hand. The two Scots moved forward, blades at the ready. Two mutineers turned on them, and they lashed out. In a moment there was a tangle of men yelling and screaming. It was a nightmare. Mary didn't know which were rebels and which were loyalists.

They were all in danger. What could *she* do? She pulled off her jacket and threw it over the cutlass of a man she recognised as a mutineer. The blade dropped to the floor, useless until disentangled. Another man lunged at Harry who veered to the side and thrust forward with his cutlass. The mutineer grunted, and fell slowly down amongst the legs and feet behind him. The first man pulled his knife free to push through the group of fighting sailors behind him. Seeing one of their leaders move back, some of the group hesitated.

'Good man! Good!' Cameron was behind them. Harry glared, panting. 'Look out! Look out!' The fighting was still going on, but it was becoming sporadic. Another crowd was forming, but of loyalists this time. Some of the rebels were moving away, sheathing their cutlasses. But Setton was still facing the rebel group, urging them on and shouting.

Cameron moved fast, shoving his way through the growing crowd. He thrust his pistol into Setton's back.

'Call them off, or you die! TRAITORS!' The last word was loud enough to reach far along the deck. More sailors came rushing up. One by one the rebels were captured and overpowered. Silent, surly, they relinquished their weapons, and were marched off.

'It's over!' Cameron settled his pistol in its holster and turned his attention to Setton, still struggling furiously with the gun captain and some of the crew. 'Take him to the hold and put him in irons! I want him for questioning.' He turned. 'Mistress – ehm – Watson! get up to the top deck. The surgeon is with the Captain and may need help.'

Her thoughts were in turmoil. Harry safe,

herself safe though aching and, exultantly in her mind, a spy defeated! Mary struggled up to the top deck where the captain was lying on the deck.

The first lieutenant was in command, yelling,

'Battle stations! Battle stations!'

Little puffs of smoke came from different ships. The French and Spanish had begun firing.

Help had arrived and the captain was being moved. She staggered on her way, the pain and terror of her capture, the mutiny and the fighting had almost stupefied her. But she told herself that others had suffered – there were worse injuries and greater pain endured. She forced herself to move, following the men carrying the Captain.

On the orlop deck, Surgeon Graham was angry.

'Do not desert your post again, Watson! Not until I give you leave.'

'Sorry, sir, it won't happen again.' She wished she could tell him what had happened, but there was no time.

CHAPTER TWENTY-SIX

ENGLAND EXPECTS EVERY MAN TO DO HIS DUTY

The signal came from Lord Nelson.

'Aye, and Scotland too,' muttered Mary. The surgeon and his assistants were steady in the orlop deck, ready for the first casualties of the battle.

The ship was sailing closer and closer towards the line of the French fleet and the wind was calming. Sailing at such an angle allowed Nelson to use the guns on both sides of the ship.

And the guns began! Gunfire, which she'd heard sporadically as the gun crews practised, now began in earnest. Noise of feet thumping along the decks, running, yells, screams, shouts. And loud bangs. Smoke eddying from the cannons swirled even into the lower decks. She looked up at the sound of more running feet down the sickbay. Harry stood at the door, finger to his lips. She ran to him.

'Oh Harry, Harry, my love, my dear love. Take care.'

'Shhh, I'm on the guns, and take my turn up there. I have to do it, lass, I have to be there, Mary. The admiral himself has set up a big signal. England – and Scotland too – expects every man to do his duty. I have to go.'

She clung to him.

'I'm glad I'm with you. I'm glad … even though the worst happens, I'm here. We're together.'

He hugged her, touched her hair.

'I have to go.'

And he turned and ran.

Feet thudded along the deck. The door flung open. Two men carrying a bleeding seaman between them set him carefully down.

'This is the first one, Watson. Here we go.'

She followed Graham to the candle table.

'Slice off his clothing here,' and Graham pointed to the shoulder. 'Undo the buttons of his coat.'

The sensitive fingers probed the bleeding gently, and the seaman groaned and twisted his head in pain.

'Swabs!' She passed warm damp cloths to the surgeon, who wiped away the blood. 'Watson, do this here for me.'

She began as gently as she could but the man twisted and turned in pain, and tried to pull away her fingers. A glance at the nearest loblolly boy brought him over.

'I'll hold him, Mr Watson.'

She continued swabbing until the wound was clean and exposed. Now what? She looked round for the surgeon. He was busy with another two – no, three men already. Dear God! This was battle!

The bleeding seemed to have stopped and she bandaged the wound. The man struggled to sit up. They helped him, and he swung his legs off the table.

'Back to battle,' he said. 'Confusion to Boney.'

'Confusion to Boney!' Mary and the other loblolly boy echoed. Confusion indeed to that dreadful tyrant, Mary thought, bringing this destruction on people.

And, as always in her thoughts, what was Harry up to right at this minute?

But she had no time to wonder. More and more men were queuing up to see the surgeon, some leaning against the deck and the tables, some lying on sails, having been dragged and lifted by their mates and some half leaning, half lying. Blood was spilling on to the deck, making it slippery, and a boy began sprinkling sand over it.

She moved between one and another man, asking, checking, swabbing, slitting clothes, pulling off boots. And still the guns were firing. The relentless noise boomed in her ears. There was no escape, nowhere she could go to hide her face, cover her ears. This was war! And she, Mary Watson from Sillery, in Fife, was right in the middle of it. She put her fingers in her ears briefly, and shook her head, to try to get rid of the noise. But it continued, even louder. Harry! How was he? What was he up to?

The ship shuddered and shook as the guns on deck fired, one after the other, simultaneously and at intervals. Feet scurried everywhere, men were shouting.

'Fire! Fire! Fire!'

And men were screaming, yelling in pain as one after the other was hurt, wounded, hit by shot or splinters.

Men staggered along the deck to have their wounds attended to as fast as possible. Down below decks, the sickbay cots and chairs were full of men, some lying, some sitting holding their arms, legs, shoulders, heads cradled in hands. Moaning, groaning and some yelling in pain.

And there was a corner for bodies. She was still sickened as she saw the pile of corpses grow, and as more bodies were added to the pile, she tried to check each face, as best she could, in case one was Harry. But the bloody battlestains disguised most of the faces. She and the other assistants were rushing everywhere. There was little time to swab cloths out: she was reaching for odd clean corners to wipe blood and grit from wounds. The water was filthy. She was cutting into fabric to expose wounds. She was shaking powder into wounds, she was bandaging. She paused to wipe her sweaty forehead with her forearm.

'Over here!' Graham barked at her. 'Swab this wound. Hold this powder. I'm taking off his arm.'

She saw men she knew from boarding the boat with them and sharing their quarters. She saw Archie Stott, grimy and grey, no longer with the Mess as cook but with the fighters. And wounded as well. His arm in a sling, his shirt grubby with blood and gunfire fall-out, Archie was no longer a young son, but a man, and a courageous fighter. His parents would be proud, no doubt.

She no longer wanted to vomit as she heard the saw bite into bone. She kept her senses as an arm or a leg dropped or rolled off into the sawdust. Graham was so skilled, the amputations took less than two minutes. She was still amazed by such ability.

A touch on her shoulder made her jump. She turned. A grey-haired man blackened with gunsmoke, reddened with dirty blood stood beside her.

'It's me, Harry, lass.'

She would never have recognised him. His left arm hung useless at his side. Blood was running down his right thigh. His shoes were caked with blood and dirt. His shirt was ripped.

She found him a space and squeezed him in between other wounded.

'Bide there until I come.'

He grinned.

'Not much else I can do. And Mary, lass … he's over there.'

Harry pointed with his good hand. Setton lay slumped against a bulkhead.

Was this the end of his scheming and spying? she wondered. Why was he not left dying in irons below decks? She went over to him. Behind her Surgeon Graham said,

'We need him alive, Watson. Thus we care for him.' So Surgeon Graham did believe in Setton's treachery, she thought.

She bent over Setton. A helpless man, once a traitor, he was to get the same treatment as the British fighting men. Had it not been for the surgeon's words, she might have ignored him. Setton's eyes opened. He recognised her, and a grim smile stretched his lips.

'Mistress Mary, despite all that's happened, I'm right glad to see you here. I have … a fondness … a kindness for you.'

'Shh.' She began to unbutton his coat, easing it away from his body where the coat and shirt were sticky with blood. His wrists were scarred with the iron handcuffs, now dangling unlocked from one hand. He winced.

'Aaaahhh.' But she had no time to waste in comfort. She had to get to the wound. She drew off the handcuffs, and got his coat manoeuvred over his wounded arm. She threw the cuffs behind her, with a loud clatter. They might never be needed again.

Turning back to Setton, she continued pulling off his bloody clothes, squeezed a swab out in a bucket of water and began to sponge off the blood. The ball had smashed into his side, and his ribs were exposed, with bits of the bone hanging loose. This was beyond her, she thought. Just clean up, and bandage lightly, and wait for the surgeon. She got up from her knees, clutching at a nearby table for support, and looked round.

Dear God, there were even more men crammed into this small area.

'Who's next?' she stammered, picking up her bucket of water.

'More water, Watson.' A loblolly boy passed her a fresh bucket and took the old one. 'Over here please.'

She nearly fell over an amputated leg on the deck. Another loblolly boy picked it up, cradling it in his arms, and ran off with it to a big bin, where there were already several amputated limbs, with the bones exposed, the threads of ligaments trailing, and the blood in some beginning to stop oozing.

She stooped over the next man. There was no time to think, no time to pause and reflect. She had to move fast. To the next man. And again another. She lost count of the number of wounded she'd seen and tried to help before the surgeon came along.

Mary hurried hither and thither, she knew not for how long. Her boots were covered in spots of blood, her own shirt was stiff with blood and vomit. Her hair hung loose, and her eyes were almost closing with tiredness but more with the horrors of seeing the wounded and their sufferings.

At one moment in the battle, Graham touched her shoulder.

'You're doing a grand job, Watson.'

'I didn't think it would be so bad,' she muttered.

'War is a dreadful thing, Mistress, to be avoided where possible.' He acknowledged her gender publicly for the first time.

She pushed a lock of hair out of her eyes.

'Invasion would be worse, sir.'

'Aye, you're right.' And Graham went off to the next wounded man in the queue.

Gradually the noise lessened. Gradually the queue of wounded diminished. Gradually the smoke diminished, blown away in the wind.

Gradually the sky returned to blue, the clouds to white, the sun shone.

'Was it over?' she wondered.

CHAPTER TWENTY-SEVEN

Late afternoon saw a light wind clearing away the last of the smoke. The surgeon's quarters were still the scene of men lying down, men sitting holding stumps of arms or legs, men pressing bandages against wounds.

But the noise had died down. Gunfire was finished, or at most sporadic. The battle was over.

And Britain had won.

But at what a cost! Hundreds of men killed over the fleet, even more wounded. And, maybe worst of all, she thought, Admiral Nelson was dead.

The door opened and Harry came in, his bandaged arm tucked into a sling. He smelt of fresh salty sea air.

Mary put a finger to her lips. He raised his eyebrows in question, and she shook her head. His face fell into a new, sad, grim expression.

'Jock?'

'Harry, is that you, man?' The whisper from the bed was hoarse, and choked.

'Aye lad, give me your hand.'

'They've done for me, Harry, the Frenchies have got me. I doubt ...' – his breath came in gasps – 'I doubt ... I'll not live till the morn.'

Mary wiped Jock's head and adjusted the torn blanket.

'Can we nae get a better blanket than this?'

Mary shook her head.

'It disnae matter ... Harry ... I just wish I'd lived to see my wee bairn. I dinnae even ken whit it is.'

Mary looked at Harry, then bent down close to Jock's face.

'You've got a wee son, Jock. We managed to get a letter frae home by the cutter.'

The dying man's face lit up. 'A wee son? My wee bairn. A son?'

'Aye, man, and they're going to call him Jock.' Harry's face was wet but his voice was steady.

Jock's eyes closed.

'Wee Jock. Wee Jock.'

'We'll all help Jeannie.' Mary's hands were gentle as she wiped Jock's face. 'She sent you a ring, I hadna managed to get it to you until just now.' She pulled off her own ring, with a questioning look at Harry. He nodded.

Jock clutched the ring with weakened fingers.

'Aye, Jeannie, I loved her. Tell her ... my love ... wee bairn ... wee Jock ...' The words tailed off, and the breathing ceased. Mary looked at Harry. Together they pulled the blanket up over their old friend's dead face. Tears spilled down her cheeks.

But there was no time to weep, to mourn, to grieve, only to try to keep up with the wounded.

Harry moved on deck again to do what he could but was soon back down.

'It's over, Mary.'

'I can't believe it.'

The fleet had taken prizes of French and Spanish ships, and many survivors had been picked out of the water. And now, they were on their way home.

'What happened to Setton?'

'Don't know.' replied Harry. 'I haven't liked to ask.'

'You're wanted in the Captain's cabin,' a voice snapped behind them.

'Aye aye, sir!' They both jumped to attention automatically.

The Captain's cabin was the grandest room Mary had ever seen, all polished wood and silverware. It seemed a thousand miles from battle.

Ewan Cameron stood by the window, and they found the wounded Captain upright at his desk, signing papers. He handed them a piece of paper each.

'These are your release papers, for both of you,' he said, smiling. 'Although, Mistress, you were not pressed and are exempt from returning to the service, a seaman is not allowed to leave the service without permission. And,' turning to Harry, 'I seem to have an exemption certificate here for you, Master Watson. I wonder how it was overlooked before.'

Mary noticed that Mr Cameron was smiling. He had managed to pass it to the Captain at last.

'But for your services,' the Captain went on, 'we might not have apprehended a traitor. Nor might we have found two other ships with mutineers on them. As we were ready for their action, we were better able to put down their little rebellion.'

'What would have happened if we had not?'

Mary burst out, forgetting she shouldn't speak up to the Captain until invited to do so.

Cameron intervened.

'With your permission, sir, I can answer that.' He turned to them. 'The document showed that Setton had orders from Napoleon to take three ships towards the French line, to try to confuse the battle plans drawn up by Admiral Nelson, and to add another ship to the French and Spanish fleet. If possible, he was to sail near the *Victory* and shoot the Admiral.'

'But wouldn't Setton himself then get shot?' asked Harry.

'Why?' added Mary. 'Why would he turn to the French?'

'Money, most likely, Mistress. Money and maybe position. For the mutineers also. A French victory might see him in a special command. And land and money for poor men, something which we all want.' Cameron hesitated. 'And yes, he might have been shot. But the effort to confuse the fleet would have been even greater with the death of Nelson *before* the battle. Killing Nelson, with the support of the mutineers on board, would have ensured him a strong position on this ship.'

'But, but,' Harry stammered, 'the uprising didn't succeed.'

'Thanks to Mistress Watson here for exposing him as a traitor early on. We had some idea of his plans, and we were ready.'

The captain intervened.

'Enough, man! We could talk over this for ever.' He smiled at them, wearily. 'These papers entitle you to leave the service of the Navy and go on your way home. They will give you free passage to London, and thence to Leith. Go well.'

'Aye aye sir!'

And they saluted as they left the cabin.

CHAPTER TWENTY-EIGHT

Their ship was detailed to go to Portsmouth, and with the relaxed atmosphere after the battle, they began to count the days until they landed. The Exemption Certificate which Mary had carried on that long journey from Fife had freed Harry, while Mary herself had been released from further service. She was still wearing her seaman's clothing, but she had let her hair down, and the sailors laughed at her when they saw her.

'What did we say that might have shocked you, Mistress?'

Mary had asked the Captain if Archie Stott could be released from the service, but he was refused permission, and told he had to fulfil his years of duty.

'I love the boats and sailing,' he said pathetically, 'but I'd fine like to be back hame.'

He managed to write a short sentence to his

parents, and Mary added to it from his dictation, saying how much he was enjoying the life. True, up to a point, she thought. When he knew she and Harry were going home, he forgot his love of sailing, wiping his eyes and sniffing.

'Men do not weep.'

'But here, you may. War is a sad, sad, business,' Mary comforted him.

Ewan Cameron frequently joined them on the deck, and told them more about the spy network than Mary at least wanted to know. His tale was one of treachery. Setton was from The Glen, and his ancestors were Jacobites loyal to the exiled royal family, resident in France, and resistant to the union of Scotland with England, and the creation of the United Kingdom. Though Charles Edward Stuart was defeated, there were certain French elements which still considered Scotland as a potential ally, and certain Scots who thought that France might help restore Scotland to independence. Mary and Harry were horrified.

'You mean ... break up the Union?'

'That's it. And that's all we need to know.' Mr Cameron turned to Mary. 'You'll be glad to get home, Mistress.'

'Yes!' Mary was emphatic. 'I want to get back to Sillery, back to a quieter life, back to my family and friends.'

Harry grinned.

'Can't see you settling down quietly, after all this,' he teased her.

On dry land at Portsmouth, they seized each other and did a wild Highland fling on the docks.

'Home! Home!' yelled Harry.

A rattle on the cobblestones made them turn. An escort party with a coach was waiting by the quayside, and coming along the gangplank, escorted by four sailors, was Setton. Dishevelled and unshaven, clothes torn, arm in a sling, he stumbled on to the quayside. He saw them and raised a fist.

'None of that!' ordered the leading seaman, pushing him along.

Mary looked at Harry.

'What'll happen to him?'

Mr Cameron joined them.

'He'll report to my Lords of the Admiralty, and, we hope, give them some useful information.'

Harry caught at her.

'He'd have killed you, lass, in a minute. Without a thought.'

She shuddered, remembering that struggle

on the stairway. But she was alive, and on her way home.

'Home, Harry, please!'

'Good luck to both of you, and you may count me as friend.' Cameron moved over to a private carriage, waving them goodbye.

'Come on, then!' yelled Harry, waving their release papers. 'What're we waiting for?'

'HOME.'

ABOUT THE AUTHOR

Beatrice Hale is Aberdeen born and bred, but now lives in New Zealand where she draws on the vibrant tales from her family history for her books for adults and children.

The inspiration for this story comes from an ancestor in Cellardyke, Fife, who was a victim of the pressgang around 1800. But his Mary wife went with him!

Look for *Ice Escape*, too, a children's adventure story based on real events in the 1930s Arctic.

www.ingramcontent.com/pod-product-compliance
Lightning Source LLC
Chambersburg PA
CBHW060805190726
48285CB00002B/549